MYTH OF PTERYGIUM

PRAISE FOR *MYTH OF PTERYGIUM*

Like all the best myths, Diego Gerard Morrison's surrealist mirror throws our own world into such sharp focus it practically draws blood. Simultaneously hallucinatory and utterly clear-eyed, *Myth of Pterygium* whirls the reader through a near-future-on-fire via the inimitable perspective of a broke poet and father-to-be as he tries to build a future for himself and his family in a city falling apart at the seams. Seeking clarity in the face of literal and figurative blindness, *Myth* asks us what evils have we inherited—familial, cultural, political, environmental—and is it too late to escape them? How can we confront the present with radical imagination when our survival often seems dependent on our perpetuation of the very systems that are destroying us? Mixing philosophy, slapstick adventure, and meditations on the writing life with encounters with tarot-card-reading matriarchs of firearm empires, *Myth* employs the high and the low and everything in between in a narrative that is remarkable for its seamless, and seemingly effortless, blend of genres and tones. But even greater than its formal inventiveness is the novel's generosity of spirit; in the midst of *Myth's* grief and uncertainty is the sense that we must live and to love not in spite of, but *because* of, existential threats on the personal and global scale. A gently terrifying, funny, and almost unbearably moving feat from an extraordinary imagination.

– MARYSE MEIJER, AUTHOR OF *THE SEVENTH MANSION*

Diego Gerard Morrison's enigmatic and sweet-humored debut is a thing all of its own. It's a poignant account of how family, self, and love come together, drift apart, and somehow—gently, miraculously—reform. It's a satire on the logic of artistic production against a background of elaborate brunches, crime of baroque violence, and no-longer-just-impending ecological collapse. It's a purgatorial evocation of a city that's forever pulling itself apart and trying to begin again, all relayed in a form and style whose reckoning with the physical will leave you looking up from the page with the world around you freshened and suddenly, newly relentless. Rich, strange, and brilliant, you won't read anything else like *Myth of Pterygium*.

–TIM MACGABHANN, AUTHOR OF *HOW TO BE NOWHERE*

Written with aberrant rhythm and a vision that is both expansive and at other times remarkably compressed, Diego Gerard Morrison's debut novel explores what lies in the center of a narrative only to discover events that unexpectedly occur on the margins. Morrison's prose style seduces the reader with its descriptive originality, while at the core of the protagonist's cognitive dissonance the flow of images is both filmic and poetic. *Myth of Pterygium* is a portrait of a young poet who resists social conformity. By the mere virtue of surrendering to time as an existential condition, where the past and present seem to collapse, the poet's spirit calls forth for the validation of human complexity. His is a miraculous analog that we all can identify as we turn the pages with wondrous pleasure.

–PHONG H. BUI, PUBLISHER AND ARTISTIC DIRECTOR, *THE BROOKLYN RAIL*

MYTH OF PTERYGIUM

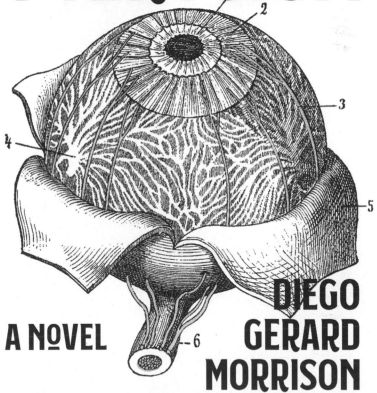

A NOVEL

DIEGO GERARD MORRISON

AUTUMN HOUSE PRESS

Pittsburgh, PA

pennsylvania
COUNCIL ON THE ARTS

Autumn House Press receives state arts funding support through a grant from the Pennsylvania Council on the Arts, a state agency funded by the Commonwealth of Pennsylvania, and the National Endowment for the Arts, a federal agency.

Cover design by Melissa Dias-Mandoly

ISBN: 9781637680292
LCCN: 2021950335

All Autumn House books are printed on acid-free paper and meet the international standards of permanent books intended for purchase by libraries.

For Lu

1

From one day to the next, my right eye is bloodshot and itchy—
unusually so.

2

"It's a pterygium. It's benign," the ophthalmologist says. "Dryness, altitude, pollution, all contribute to it." She opens her drawer and hands me eye drops. "Use these. Twice a day."

3

"It's benign," I tell my wife through the phone. "I'll just look like the undead." The blare of Mexico City traffic muffles her response while through our Ford Bronco's dust-streaked windshield, the thick cloud of pollution renders the sky underexposed, Baudelairean.

4

My wife is leaning her pregnant belly over the slant of her drafting table when I walk into our duplex; her eyes are pensive, and she's breathing loud as she works on the design for one of her utopias, an urbanist's dream of a sustainable city. "Sure that's good for the baby?"

She turns, ready to craft a response, but falters, "Oh," she says, "your eye."

5

She carries on with her work, slicing paper trees, gluing them to her eco mock-up, and I climb to our second-story bedroom to find a new email from my present, and only, client, a real would-be writer: *I need these edited ASAP, feel free to charge a rush fee.* I breathe out slowly and look out the window, where elevated particles lend a static-like quality to the air. I rub my bad eye with exceptional pressure as if, like Oedipus, I want to gouge it out.

6

Effacing lines, making notes in the margins, leaving a flood of virtual red ink over the Would-Be-Writer's text—a rambling paragraph about the death of his twin brother at the moment of birth. My red lines on the white page run like the red veins in the would-be white of my right eye, which I rub again, wincing, and flinching as I fully reopen it to find the famous writer—the man missing an arm, a hook in its place, wearing an overcoat despite the humid weather—walking his two mutts across the ready-made screen of my window until he's out of frame.

7

The sight of the Famous-Armless-Writer makes me quit editing and click open my botched poetry collection. The first several poems, the bits that go out to agents and publishers, must be eye-catchers. A bit of dramatic irony to render enough mystery, a hook for the reader like the one in place of the famous writer's lost arm. My wife catches me working on my collection and approaches me from behind. "*Poems?*" she asks with a sardonic pitch to her voice. "Won't pay our looming bills." She runs a smooth hand over her convex belly.

I turn and meet her eyes. "But isn't that the dream? Have poems pay for our bills?"

8

The pediatrician's office has pink carpeting and blue walls, is filled to the brim with stuffed animals, and is loud with iPads playing cartoons on a continuous loop. My wife's belly boasts a beautiful curvature and shivers as the doctor spreads gel over it with the ultrasound's probe. "Nice and healthy," he says, "went from a mango to a melon in only a few weeks."

I run a trembling finger over the mercurial image on the screen, which shows traces of movement, a blob somewhat shaped like a baby, conquering more of my wife's uterus. "Steady growth, just like our expenses," I say, turning to my wife, who can't rid the smile of awe from her face. There is a glint in the browns of her eyes despite the city's gray light.

9

My credit card is refused. The swipe reader beeps prematurely and spits out the void receipt. The cashier shakes her head oh so mildly. "Running low?" my wife asks.

Already starting to dash, I turn to her. "I'll get some cash downstairs."

The connecting dots on the ATM screen wink long and drowsy while the view behind the glass shows a glimpse of our urban dystopia: traffic jam brake lights, strings of car exhaust rising to invisibility. Finally—reluctantly almost—the bills come out.

Back upstairs, the money switches hands, and my wife hands me a bottle of eye drops the pediatrician gave her for me during my absence. "Try these. That thing in your eye, it's alive, getting bigger and bloodier by the day."

10

The drive home comes to a standstill, the inside of our decrepit Ford Bronco sweltering. With every forward jolt, the car coughs and whines. "What's next?" my wife asks. "The wheels will come off while we're actually moving?"

The radio isn't on, but there is still a faint scratch of static; the CD player is busted, so my wife pulls out my laptop to play something from my iTunes under rush hour bedlam. The laptop quivers as she balances it over the swell of her belly, and when we inch forward, the Bronco shudders and the engine dies. Reigniting, I step heavily onto the pedal, making the engine belt a wild roar. Wincing, my wife says, "Maybe sell it for parts, whatever we can get?" With that, the car jerks forward and my MacBook slides off her belly. She lifts her brows as she picks it up, showing me a shattered-glass wound on the right side of the screen.

11

The crack on my laptop screen has slowed down my work. "I need a new one," I tell my wife, who, upon hearing my complaint, walks up to me and hugs me around my neck, her skin giving off the smell of her pregnancy cravings: pork rinds and spicy peppers.

"We need tons of stuff; your editing income and my maternity leave can only cover so much. Maybe it's time you get a *job* job, join the family biz. Nothing is scarce there."

I turn to face her. "You want me to sell guns for a living?"

"You'll be just like Rimbaud," she says, a sly grin tugging at the corners of her lips. "Sexy, isn't it? You kinda have the piercing, blank gaze of his youth anyway." She pauses. "Except for that red eye."

"No," I shake my head, "Rimbaud was already a legend before he started with guns."

She shrugs. "Still sexy if you ask me."

12

The news on TV can best be described as the bastard child of current events and slasher films. "If it's not gore, it doesn't make prime time," my wife says, lowering the volume with the remote and walking off to bed. The gunfire on the screen makes me wonder if my mother's gun enterprise is feeding all this drug violence. I turn the TV off and follow my wife to bed, asking her if she really wants me to sell guns. *Rimbaud!* Ah, the cunning in her words!

"You'd be a salesman, not an executioner."

"I don't know," I say, letting out a long and heavy sigh. I lie down next to her in bed and place a hand on her belly, which rises and falls with her breath.

"You really think your mom and brother are responsible for all the blood?"

We fall silent, but then there's the suggestion of movement inside her, followed by a blatant kick. My wife squirms and sits up while a rush of dopamine tingles in my skull. "Holy shit," I say, and we both place our hands over it. "She really *is* coming, isn't she?"

The text I'm editing for the Would-Be-Writer is full of telling details about his wealth, which makes it all the more baffling why he can never pay me on time. *We have always been a fortunate family,* it reads, *in material terms,* and goes on to narrate how he came to be, alongside his stillborn twin, in the most expensive and specialized maternity hospital Houston had to offer and how, with time, it felt like being born *lacking a limb,* which led him to therapy since the age of six with the most renowned Lacanian psychoanalyst in Mexico City. I click open my email to reattach the latest invoice, writing up the amount in bold, **$1,891**, good enough for one visit to the pediatrician and a small number of groceries—"I need habaneros and chicharrón, baby cravings getting surreal." I click "send" and the computer emits a sound conveying either flight or speed, and I sit there, seething before my damaged screen, until it goes black. My face reflected there seems deeply shadowed, but I can see the thing in my eye has gained territory. The white, meaty tissue is now shaped like a sharp wedge and has bloody veins running through it, threatening to overtake my cornea.

14

My right eye is sore and damp after dispensing a few of the pediatrician's eye drops into it; I curl up in bed next to my wife. Again, her skin gives off the food stall scent of habanero-smeared chicharrón. "This thing in my eye, it's killing me. Can't even watch TV."

"You need a second opinion."

"A new eye, perhaps."

"Doctors can sometimes fuck up."

"She said it was benign. Maybe that's all I need to hear."

"I'm sure it is, but there might be a way to get rid of it, like surgery, maybe."

I roll away from her, breathe out, and stare at the light-washed ceiling. Beside me, she breathes out too, with strain. "Oh shit," she says, "move over." She springs from bed and runs to the bathroom. I can hear her through the wall, her body moving through space. Then comes her barfing, followed by a sloshing sound. I walk to her aid only to realize she didn't make it to the toilet—the vomit is surprisingly odorless and spreads in a creamy red over the floor like the wedge-shaped intrusion over the white of my right eye.

15

The second opinion with the new ophthalmologist, the new eye drops, the prescribed sunglasses, plus the latest visit to the pediatrician add up to way more than what the Would-Be-Writer owes me. "We need to find a solution," my wife says. "Babies cost a million dollars this day and age." She whistles while shaking her head, then gets into the car.

It takes three choking attempts to get the Bronco's engine revving, and I catch my wife lifting her brows before I slip on my new sunglasses. Once we are out of the parking lot, the polarized lenses shade the polluted city with a dark, eerie tinge, like Chris Marker's *La Jetée*, and my wife begs me again to take a job with my mother. "Part-time, at least."

"I wish she would just sell the business, cash her offspring out."

Once parked outside our building, we run into the Famous-Armless-Writer walking his hideous-looking mutts, his black hood casting a shadow over his face. My wife cringes out of their way and shoots them a smile that might suggest pity or fear. "He scares the shit out of me," she says when the writer is out of earshot. "Like Holy Death lives next door."

"Do you know who that is?" I say, but she is already way ahead of me, leaving me to wonder if the writer's ravaged look might serve as a favor for a symbolist writer's career.

16

My brother picks up on the second ring. "Well, well, well," he says. "I can't believe my eyes . . . or my ears . . . it's been a while."

"Yeah, no, how are you? Everything all right?"

"All right, yeah, good," he says. In the background, there is the blast of gunfire.

"Always working I see."

"You know me," and then the swift stutter of semiautomatic rounds.

"So, the business is going well, I guess, bulking up the profits, are you?"

"Business is good. I won't lie. There's always gun demand in this country of ours."

A flash of the scenes I saw on the news last night runs through my mind: the murdered men and women of the drug war, our armed forces, faux stoic, holding our family's guns.

"Still there?" my brother asks after my silence.

"Yeah," I say, rubbing my bad eye, which is surely as bloody as the corpses shown on TV. "So, how's Mother? Still thinking of selling the business? Cash us out? Live in plenty?"

"Tired of la bohème, are you?" he says, and then quiets as if expecting me to lash back. After the lengthy pause, he adds, "Mom's good, wants to see us both soon actually. I'll keep you posted." There's another gun blast in the background before he hangs up.

17

The wound on the screen of my computer is leaking at a sure yet barely discernible pace, like a busted pen in a trouser pocket. I have to shrink my Firefox window so it avoids the spill. After a few minutes of looking at pictures of Rimbaud in Ethiopia, my email pings with an update in my bank balance. The Would-Be-Writer has finally paid me, but the balance is still lower than my credit card debt. Luckily, a few minutes later, my email pings again: another message from him with yet longer blocks of text: *After close consideration, I think this text best suits the form of a creative essay. I'm attaching a proposal for you to perk up. I'll get some big names to collaborate. It could be a great book, and I want you to be my editor.*

I paste his text into a Word document and set the font to eight-point so the screen's hemorrhage won't get in the way. After my first skim, it seems like he's putting less effort into constructing full sentences, rather just typing impetuous thoughts onto the page. What he needs is more akin to a ghostwriter, not an editor. Overcome with dread, I look away to the action behind my computer through my window where, in a flare of rare sunlight, the Famous-Armless-Writer is picking up runny dog shit with a plastic bag over his only hand off the sidewalk. *Perfect collaborator*, I think, and from downstairs, my wife's voice reaches me as she slides the window shut, her words loud: "That's just fucking disgusting. Don't ever get me a pet!"

Fecal matter on the loose, broken down to microscopic sizes, is just one of the hundreds of types of toxic particles we chilangos inhale on a daily basis. Add to that the broken muffler fumes from a city with a population of twenty-four million, the pollution from factories lining the outskirts of the city, the smoke from frying pots and pans of street food stalls on every corner, the ashy puffs from the volcanoes, all of it forming the cloud of smog that constantly hangs over the valley. Stretching my eye open in front of the mirror, I tell my wife, "I look like a monero." She is sitting on our torn couch, leafing through Homero Aridjis's novel, *La Leyenda de Los Soles*. "I could sure make some dough lathering up windshields on Insurgentes." I approach her to show her my eye up close.

She looks into it briefly, then returns to her book. "I don't think there's anything to worry about as long as you can see out of it."

"But look at this," I say, rubbing my eye with more force than I should, partially soothing the itch at its inner corner.

"I know. It looks like shit. But nobody cares about how it looks."

"This isn't about vanity. This is about being functional in the world."

"The only thing we are not, my love," she says, her fiery brown eyes resting on the white, dog-eared cover of her book, "is functional."

"Hard to disagree with that one," I say, and she shoots me a brazen smile.

19

My new ophthalmologist's office is so sharply designed, with the smoothest of black leathers and the coziest of forty-watt lights, that my only true desire is to lounge on her fine furniture and stare out the fifteenth-story panoramic windows at the murky, yellowing sky hanging over the city. She wears round, tortoise-shell glasses and a corduroy blazer. Her reddish hair falls straight and luminous to her shoulders. The whites of her eyes are, indeed, white, beautiful, enough for me to feel a slash of envy stinging in my abdomen.

She has me sit on a black leather settee that might better be-fit Freudian analysis, asking about sensory cues in my right eye: the tacky corner, the irritation, the dryness, the twitching—or is it a throbbing?—the wedge-shaped tissue with a will of its own spreading and reaching for my cornea. "I wouldn't say the pain is profound," I tell her as she scribbles on a notepad that is also black leather. "It's just hard to make good first impressions."

She nods and writes at the same time, then directs me with a wave of her pen to the metal apparatus where I rest my chin so she can shoot light and a puff of air into my eye.

"Yes," she says, pulling away. "It is a pterygium. A condition ailing those living between the tropics, at high altitude—Mexico City isn't quite the ideal place for you."

"I was told it's benign."

"It is. But it can block your vision if it grows large enough."

"Will you give me eye drops too? Some really strong ones?"

"The only way to remove it is surgery. I go into your eye, but then it's gone for good."

20

The tips of my fingers are sweaty over the keyboard, leaving oily spots with every peck. The Would-Be-Writer's text has turned out to be part of an ill-conceived project: he wants to talk about his stillborn brother in a pseudo-magical-realist sort of way, as if he had grown up alongside him, as if his presence was some sort of ghost-pain, the amputation of his hypothetical better half—his better *self*, even—which he calls, for reasons both unfathomable and unknown, a *binomial shadow.*

Despite my impaired vision, I find no difficulty letting loose in the margins: *this opening deserves full sentences and an active voice / at which point in time are you writing this? / could the use of second-person narration help these clunky shifts between first and third? / render your characters through sympathy and complexity / are you thinking in terms of artistic mystery?*

The proposal he came up with aims to attract writers who have used amputation, the broken appendage, and yes, *the intellectual prosthetic* as a theme in their work. Skimming down the document, I can't help but notice the Famous-Armless-Writer's name in bold, he who roams outside my window, at the very end of the virtual page.

On the side of my screen with the black leak, now taking the shape of an unknown continent, I catch the image of my bad eye. Is my pterygium blocking part of my eyesight? Will I have to undergo surgery? I try imagining myself with only one eye, one made of glass in the place of the one removed, or wearing an eyepatch, a look that could well boost my writing career, maybe even save me from more dreary gigs like this one.

21

Phone in hand, staring at my brother's WhatsApp message asking me to call him, I pace around the duplex. I stop and look out the windows, the sunbeams weak in the city's awful ash. A hazy strip wavers at street level, wobbling over the buildings and cars barely visible through the smog. The bad air even coats the seat of a black plastic couch abandoned on the sidewalk, its seat peeling, its arms covered in a sallow film of who knows what.

I dial his number, and yet again, he picks up after the second ring.

"Ah," he says, "finally, you call."

"Busy days," I say, trying to calculate the pacing of my words to come off nonchalant.

My wife figures out I'm talking to my brother. For a moment, she stands in front of the open window, in a lit halo of pollution, and then she's straight onto me.

"So," my brother says and pauses, as if there was a reason to stretch out the suspense.

"So," I say, as my wife mouths words to me slowly, none of which I can make out.

"Yes," he says, "the gun matriarch wants to see us both."

"She does, does she?" I say and pause. "What might she want?"

"Just wants us to meet her at El Harar tomorrow at five in the afternoon."

Just the prospect of this sets off a throbbing in my chest and streams of cold sweat under my armpits. My wife is following me around. When I hang up, she gives me an enquiring look.

"My mom wants to see me and Alex tomorrow," I tell her. "That's all."

She breathes out, allowing her shoulders to sag. Behind the window, the Famous-Armless-Writer is sitting on the abandoned couch, feeding his dogs from his only hand.

22

At first, there's nothing but pines against the backdrop of an adobe wall leading to the driveway to El Harar—my childhood home, now turned into the headquarters of our family's gun-dealing enterprise.

Then there's gentle, wet wind, a timid drizzle pearling on the Bronco's dust-streaked windshield. My brother's platinum Audi A6 is parked in the driveway, glimmering under the gray light. I cut the Bronco's engine once I'm right behind his car and get out to no sound except for the crunch of gravel beneath my feet: the suburb's attempt at full silence. Even though we are only a few miles outside the city, the thin, unpolluted air flows in, cleansing my lungs. All this purity. Could my pterygium be retreating too?

I stoop to look into the car's side mirror, wincing as I lift my sunglasses to my forehead, fantasizing about whiteness, even partial, in my right eye.

23

The fantasy shatters immediately though; there's no way to reverse the damage done. In the mirror I still find that bloody wedge: resilient, red veins running across it. From my trouser pocket, I fish out my eye drops and squirt a gush into my right eye. I wince and rub, then look into the mirror again to no avail. When the watery blur recedes, the door to the house swings open. "Ah, late as you always tend to be," my brother says, emerging from the house, the faint smell of coffee escaping from behind him. He leads me in as if I don't know my way around but then stops, holds me by the shoulders and peers into my eyes.

"Still bloodshot?" I ask.

"What on earth happened to it?" he says, his forehead furrowed.

"Pterygium," I give him a slight shrug, trying to convey normality.

"Pterygium," he repeats, slightly nodding, but then turns away. "Come on, we've been waiting for you for a while now."

I follow him past the wide arch that divides the dining room from the living room, our steps becoming noiseless over the long Persian rug until I stop at a crackling feeling under my soles. Looking down, I find the rug littered with rice and coffee beans, a trail that leads to the far end of the living room where the skylight shoots a slanted beam of light over my mother sitting in her favorite chair, a charro-style lounger fitted with the same leather as the one used on the grips of her high-end guns. The brightness bathing her from above does not really suit her: it illuminates a thick blue vein in the shape of a leafless tree branch along her cheekbone, it makes the white strands in her hair glimmer, and it highlights the depth around her eyes. The coffee beans sprinkled around her chair are like empty bullet shells at her feet.

She stands when I'm right in front of her, shifting the rice and coffee underfoot, and offers the now-expected cold kiss on both cheeks. "Hard to get you to El Harar lately," she says, sitting back down, stretching her arm and showing me to the larger couch in the room.

"Well, there's no real reason for me to come," I say, allowing my rear to sink in the soft cushion of the couch. "I'm busy all the time, the coming child, you know, the lot of it."

The mention of a grandchild forces a subtle smile on her face, but my brother is quick to let out a huff of air next to me to erase it.

"Well," he says, sitting down, his face in the direction of my mother. "We're here now. What did you want to tell us?"

She drops a hand over the armrest towards the floor, running two fingertips over the rice and coffee. My brother and I know it's best not to ask and wait in silence for an elaboration.

"We've been back and forth over this crucial decision, and we are basically split." She pauses, making eye contact with both of us. "And we've had offers for all this," she says, making circular movements with her uplifted index finger, conveying what seems to mean vastness. "In fact, I received the juiciest of offers only last week: the federal government is looking to bid for our company."

Immediately, her words kindle something warm in my viscera. It lingers in me for some seconds, then gently drifts out of my body. Has the time come? Will she sell? Will she cash us out? Beside me, my brother begins a slight jitter of his leg, and a pulse runs along the base of the couch. He watches my mother pick up a handful of rice and coffee.

"All this," she shifts the grains and beans in her cupped palm, "is the remnants of clairvoyance."

"Clairvoyance," I say with a trailing voice while my brother places a palm on his forehead and shuts his eyes before slowly shaking his head.

"Alex," my mother says curtly. Alex: a name that is both hers and my brother's.

"Come on," I say, flicking his knee, already imagining a life in an apartment of my own, one with a room for my daughter, a crib and a mobile over it, a new computer, waving off the Would-Be-Writer's demands in exchange for meager money, a clear eye after surgery, the time to write poems. I slap the nape of my brother's neck so he comes out of his stupor and order him, "Listen to what she has to say."

He raises his hands in defense and moves farther away from

me. Once reaching what he deems to be a safe distance, he turns to my mother. "I don't want you to sell. This has become my life as it has been yours; you groomed me for it, and I can't do without it."

"Since when do you talk like a soap opera star?" my mother responds. "I actually *don't* want to sell."

The warm feeling that I had in my gut is slowly replaced by a sensation of hollowness, and above us, rain patters steadily onto the skylight.

"Then why am I here?" I ask. "What exactly has changed?"

"The tarot avowed, told me I shouldn't sell, that this house, this business, it needs me, for the time being, fit to face the upcoming storm."

"Cards? Upcoming storm . . . " I repeat, and I'm not sure if I lay it out as a question or a resigned sigh.

"The cards," says my brother, suddenly jovial. "What cards?"

My mother entwines her hands over her lap and tells us that once the offer for the business came in, she summoned the clairvoyant who drew the cards, who cleansed the house with rice and coffee, who saw into the future, who delivered the news of death circling this family, and at the word *death,* my brother pales.

"Yes," my mother looks straight into his face. "Someone bearing our name will die this calendar year. Holy Death came up after the Fallen Tower.

I notice myself shaking my head mildly, absentmindedly.

"A matter of numerology," my mother says, "the one real divinity."

"This is just splendid," I say.

Now my brother slaps my knee. "Listen to what she has to say," but my mind is as hazy as my eyesight.

"I wanted you to know that's why I'm keeping the business for now, the *tower,*" my mother says. "If *I* die, you two can fight to shreds about it, or who knows, maybe you'll decide to be brothers in arms." She chuckles, clears her throat, then continues in a more serious tone. "If you die, Alex," she looks at my brother, "we can sell—God knows that's what your brother wants." She pauses to pick up more of the remnants of clairvoyance. Then, turning to me and tossing me a coffee bean, she says, "If you die, we can keep it, and Alex can be the gun lord he believes himself to be."

My brother shakes his head, and I begin to feel weak, light-headed. My eyesight alternately dims and brightens. It takes me a minute to emerge from the sudden daze, for things around me to gain full definition and to readjust to the glaring light in the room.

"Fuck," I say, letting the coffee bean fall on the rug. "I think I need you to give me a job, then, in your tower."

My brother leans forward to look at me, and my mother slowly raises her head, furrows of confusion lining both their foreheads—an obvious gesture of biological inheritance.

"I'm broke," I say, fully reclining my back on the couch. "I'm in debt, and I need you to give me a job, effective right fucking now."

"Calm down," my mother says. "Language!"

"Get a load of this bullshit," my brother cuts in, finally leaving behind his soap opera shtick. "Like you can just waltz right in, like the door's always open."

"So, the firstborn finally wants a slice," my mother says.

"I need a slice, any slice I can get."

"Wait—I've put in all I have for years," my brother says. "You've ridiculed it all your life in favor of your poems."

"Alex!" my mother scolds. Then, turning to me, she says, "It's a *family business*," lingering on every syllable. "You can begin next month. We do need someone to be in charge of ammunition sales."

My brother cranes his neck in the direction of my mother, slowly.

"But I need it now. I need the money now. Perhaps if I can get an advance payment, a signing bonus or what have you."

My brother's response to this is something like a spit of incredulity, a string of saliva hanging from his lower lip, which he swiftly wipes away.

"I can't do that for you," my mother says.

"OK, a loan? I've already agreed to work for you."

"You just asked," my brother screams, "because you have nowhere else to turn."

"I can't give you a loan," my mother tells me.

On that, I abruptly stand and walk around the room in desperation, catching sight of the Bronco behind the window, slanted streaks of rain bursting on its grimy bodywork. "Just give me some money. Keep my car as a deposit."

My mother frowns, and my brother laughs, bitter and long. When he's done, a long silence like a bracket tightens around us, the patter of the rain growing loud and urgent on the skylight. I look around the space, my childhood home, now turned into an armory, the walls I'll be surrounded by again.

"Fine," my mother says, her voice coming loud over the rain. "I'll take your car, but I'll buy it from you, for good."

My brother turns to her again, openmouthed this time.

"Alex," my mother says, "relax. We can find a use for it, and you know it." She taps the armrests of the chair with both hands and stands. "Get him the cash," she tells my brother "Thirty grand," and turning to me, "take it or leave it, son."

"I think we know the answer to that already." I fling her the keys, which jingle in the air and catch a glint of pale daylight before landing on her palm.

My brother follows her to the next room but stops at the door. "Just wait for me outside," he tells me. "I figure you'll be needing a ride, too."

"Indeed, I will," I tell him, adding a tinge of his soap opera attitude to my words, already walking through the litter of rice and coffee, then past the door to wait under the portico, saving myself from the rain, which beats onto the ground, giving off the smell of wet soil and warm gravel. Waiting there, I text my wife, *Je est un autre.*

She responds immediately with a laughing emoji, *does this mean you took a job???*

My brother's Audi swings by, thick beads of rain rolling over its metallic skin. I sink into the warm leather seat, into the new car smell. As we drive off, I glimpse the passing image of my decrepit Bronco parked before the adobe walls of El Harar.

24

On our way back, my brother's car glides noiselessly on the toll highway. The dimming sky hides the cloud of smog that hangs over the city with its nightly shroud.

My pockets are thick with a wad of cash, *gun money,* like my brother said when he handed it to me, *drizzled with blood*—his final words, it seems, for he hasn't said another one since. His eyes remain fixed on the highway in front of us.

Coffee and rice are scattered on the car's carpet, the few bits that were embedded in our soles. I'm on the verge of asking him when Mother turned so superstitious but keep quiet to avoid a confrontation. Could all this nonsense be real, though? A death in the family, the end of a bearer of our name—the family name she gave us in the absence of a father. Tarot readings *have* been accurate in the past; there is history there to account for it. Not to mention Holy Death, the forbearing watchman, standing stoic next to the Fallen Tower.

When we reach the tollbooth, my brother turns to me but stays silent.

"Yes, Alex?"

"Contrary to what you might believe, the road isn't a social service."

I nod, looking ahead.

"Hand me a bill, perhaps, from those swollen pockets of yours."

I hand him one of my thousand-peso bills for the toll, and he doesn't bother returning the change, rather slips it straight into his blazer pocket.

Ahead of us, Mexico City is an endless cluster of quivering lights, a bottleneck of hundreds of cars in the coming distance. As soon as we hit a standstill, my phone emits its bone-tickle in my pocket: the Would-Be-Writer calling, asking about his newest paragraphs.

"I don't know if I can keep working for you," I respond, turning to my brother, who is leaning his head on his fist, his elbow steadily resting on the car's open window. "I've been obligated to take a real job."

"Fuck that," the Would-Be-Writer responds. "You have to stick to it. I'll throw in more money. This'll be a big book. Don't blow this opportunity. Take the chance to make some connections. You fancy yourself a writer too, don't you?"

My initial urge is to hang up on him, but I linger on. He then adds that he is in *advanced conversations* with the Famous-Armless-Writer about their potential collaboration.

"The man with a hook for an arm?"

"Yes, do you understand what that means?"

I'm on the verge of telling him the Famous-Armless-Writer is my neighbor but instead only come up with demands: "Make me an offer I can't refuse," I say and hang up.

My brother shakes his head in disapproval, looking ahead to the dwindling road.

Silence recaptures us as we make our way deep into the city, the traffic confining us, forcing him to drop me off a few blocks from my home.

Coming into our duplex, to the sight of my wife's uncovered belly, I feel something like a sharp stab in the abdomen, a cooling of my skin. Is my coming daughter a part of this family already, a bearer of the name?

"What's wrong?" my wife says. "You're pale as a ghost."

Holding the back of my head, I walk straight to her and lie face down over her lap.

"Oh, don't worry," she says, "it'll be temporary. You'll see." She rubs my back. "Just something to get us started." She runs a hand over her belly. "Just so we can get her off to the proper start. You'll be back to poetry in no time."

25

It's not hard to tell where the tangled elements of the dream came from, but nonetheless, I wake from it gasping for air. In the abyss of my sleep, I was trying for a coarse blend of bullets in my coffee grinder, the water gurgling to a boil next to me, my

French press ready to be filled with our signature family lead. But the grinder couldn't cope with my mother's bullets, and it began hissing out smoke, just like the one that rises off a cannon after a blast.

The sweat from my pores feels warm, but it bathes me in a goose-bumped shiver as soon as I remove the covers. Beside me, my wife is sleeping belly down, her face sunken deep into the pillow, eliciting a quicker heartbeat in my chest.

I reach over and shake her awake.

"What?" she calls out in alarm, then turns, wiping dry drool from the corners of her mouth. "What's happening?"

"What are you doing?"

"I was *sleeping*," the italics audible in her voice. "What the hell is wrong?"

"You were sleeping on your belly. You shouldn't sleep belly down. That's not good for the baby. You could be crushing her."

"She's fine. Chill. We do need the sleep, you know."

I breathe in, the air harsh in my lungs. "I was having my family's bullets for coffee in my dream."

She lets her body relax over the mattress again, breathing long, relieved. "Talk about the immediate workings of your unconscious."

"I was going to drink it. I'm sure of it, but the bullets couldn't be ground."

"Just come back to bed, sounds like nonsense to me."

I nod, "A dream of stupid sorrow." I run my hands through my hair. "It still scared the living shit out of me."

"Doesn't really sound that scary to be honest."

"No, I know, but I felt a hollowness inside me. I felt empty, you know?"

She groans in affirmation.

"I just hope everything's OK," I say, giving her belly a gentle poke. "You're sure she's fine. Everything feels normal in there?"

"We're *fine, swell*, good *and* healthy. Now come back to bed." She turns and spoons one of our pillows.

"I can't sleep like this, all stressed out," I say, and head to the bathroom to put on her fleecy robe that only descends to a miniskirt length on me.

After a sour-smelling piss, I switch on the lights and stare at my face in the mirror. My pterygium is as red and invasive as I've seen it, and I linger there for some seconds.

Walking back out, I fish out the now twenty-nine thousand pesos I got for our car from my trouser pockets, thinking this money should go to the upfront payment of every remaining visit to the pediatrician and the removal of this thing in my eye.

I descend to our lower story and put on some real coffee; there is a rare silence on the streets.

Pouring the first cup, a bloodshot dawn creeps through our window, and the updraft of pollution surrounding the valley is like the brownish steam rising from my cup. I sit before my leaking computer, staring at the scraps of my symbolist poetry collection, determined, as if I was indeed something in the likes of Rimbaud, to turn silence into words.

26

I return to bed midmorning, as the tenuous glow of our polluted atmosphere washes into our duplex, and sleep for two hours or so.

When I rise again, my mouth like cotton, I find my wife sitting in front of my open computer, reading from whatever I wrote this morning, the black leak encroaching over a good part of the virtual page.

She turns, raising two thumbs. "This is good, Arthur."

"Arthur?" I say, and pause for skeptical effect. "Not sure if this alias is a compliment or just sheer irony."

"The writing does seem *very* Rimbaud," she says, with an even heavier ironic tone.

Wincing at her, my laugh is so defeatist it makes her laugh in return.

"No, but seriously, I love it, quality material here. I like the white space, the growing word saturation."

I slowly nod at her, weighing the honesty of her words.

"The question is, who actually wants to read symbolist poetry in this day and age?"

"Ah. Touché."

"I like it though, this new method, work by day, write by night."

"Temporary, remember?"

"We'll see about that." She rises from the desk. "Now up and at 'em. Pediatrician's appointment, yeah?"

With gentle hands, she shoves me in the direction of our closet and turns on the lights inside it, which spray down, white and blinding.

27

Out on the street, the air is particulate and streams painfully into my bad eye; I rub, hard, making my vision as hazy as the atmosphere. Behind this double shroud, I can make out my wife jerking her neck around, looking for our Bronco; she then turns the corner to look for it some more. She only meets my eyes when our Uber pulls up with blinking yellow lights and I lead her toward it.

"Care to explain?"

From my pocket, I slip out the thick wad of cash. "Sold it, like you always wanted."

Her eyes are wide and unblinking, her mouth slightly parted, but she allows me to help her into the car. There seem to be words on the tip of her tongue, but after a stutter and then a hesitation, all she manages to say is "To be continued."

"Yeah, good idea," I say, still rubbing my eye, searching my pockets for my sunglasses to block the glare.

28

It's the usual drill at the pediatrician's office. My wife is prepped for the ultrasound while I pay for all our remaining visits with my *gun money*. When I step into the pink and blue room, the pediatrician shakes my hand with a tighter grip than I would like and holds it while staring at my right eye. "Did you use those drops I sent?"

I nod.

"Maybe there's no remedy," he says with a laugh. "Maybe this is just the way your eye is going to be now."

I try a calculated chuckle, then say, "I'm getting surgery, removing it for good. Can't wait to get rid of those shameless stares like yours."

He laughs again. "You'll be fine. Much higher stakes here, right?"

He places the ultrasound's probe on my wife's belly, and immediately, the image on the screen comes alive, an image made of pure silvery light against a blackened backdrop—my daughter floating in her gelatinous dwelling.

A shiver skates down my spine as I watch my wife's eyes water, their bright brown irises beaming behind a film of tears.

"Loving it," the pediatrician says. "Papaya-sized, perfect. Almost oven-ready."

My wife sighs, relieved, and I breathe out too, a mild stream of serotonin rushing through my brain.

"One concern though," the pediatrician says, "seems like she's in a horizontal position," and he circles my daughter on the screen with a virtual yellow highlighter. "See that?" he says, dividing his sight between us. "We want her turning soon, so she can make that valiant dive, headfirst, out into the world."

29

The Uber ride back is full of frustrating twists and turns. Every main avenue seems to be clogged, and the driver, ignoring the savvy solutions offered by his navigation app, looks for his own creative outlet, a side street that might free us from this jam. Every two blocks, we come to a dead end and have to return to the main avenue.

Holding my wife's hand, I can feel her rapid pulse in her fingers. Our stares back and forth are caught somewhere between hope, melancholia, and an underlying tenderness.

I'm also nervous, a broken record of sorts—*she'll be fine*; *this is normal; she'll be with us in no time*—but the racket in the back of my head keeps returning to the vague idea of my mother's psychic: the death of the bearer of our name, a Fallen Tower, Holy Death holding her swinging scythe.

When we're finally dropped off outside our building, we find a white, rundown Volkswagen bug parked right in front. The Famous-Armless-Writer and his two dogs are all sleeping inside it. While he looks so still he could be dead, the two dogs are emitting a joint, unearthly snore.

The car seats are a maze of hair, black and white, covering most of the torn leather interior. The open window lets out the wafting stench of wet dog, a sick air that flows out and merges with the ever-present pollution.

My wife turns to me with a tightened face of revulsion.

"You think he's OK?" I ask her, but she's already walking ahead, her face barely turned in my direction.

"Just come inside," she says and vanishes into our building.

30

The blood on TV, the corpses, the rising death count, the people unaccounted for in this country—a narrative that somehow draws you in. Like with fiction and poetry, current events in this hard-boiled, grind-house country of ours have only a few variations on the same theme, a few shades under which our gray light can be cast, a few slants of the truth. It's becoming hard to tell this evening news from the one the day prior and the one before that; the events are the same every day: the death of an anonymous name, a new face on a frayed MISSING PERSON poster.

My wife's wide eyes make me realize I've been mumbling this incoherent train of thought out loud.

"Interior monologue, Arthur?"

Even in the dark room with intermittent flashes of blue light from the TV, I can tell she sees the blush on my skin, and it steals a glum smile from her.

"True poet always at work?"

"Guess so. I was just thinking about how desensitized we are, how we can keep on watching all this vile shit on TV without any effect."

She nods, her face serious now. "Remember the old us?" she says, turning to look at her stomach. "We promised we'd never bring a child into this hell."

I turn to her and nod while on the screen a forensic team retrieves dead bodies from a clandestine pit—more victims of our ongoing war on drugs. We stare until the news goes to commercials. Then the press of a button plunges us into the full darkness of our room.

31

The following visit to the pediatrician hints at marginal improvement. Our daughter has resumed a sitting position, hands meeting above the umbilical cord, her bum sticking out into a *frank breech*, but she has luckily forgone what the pediatrician now calls *the posture of an astronaut floating through zero gravity*. The task ahead: getting her to fully turn in the next few weeks.

"I love improvement," the pediatrician says, waving us good-bye and giving us a thumbs up. "We're here for improvement."

What doesn't show any traces of improvement is my pteryg-ium, rather it worsens by the day. The cream-white tissue with red veins cutting across it draws more disgusted and fearful stares from my wife, acquaintances, and passersby alike. During our traffic-riddled Uber ride home, I call and schedule its removal. I'm asked to recite the numbers on my credit card to complete the booking.

"Cheers for white eyes," the receptionist says when payment goes through, her voice over the phone machine-like, perfect.

"Yes, cheers for the whites of our eyes."

My wife turns to me with one lifted brow, causing me to hang up.

"They're weird at that office," I say. "Can't quite tell what it is about them."

"And how much will our beloved pterygium be setting us back?"

"Couple of grand. We should be fine until my first gun pay-ment, at least."

"Are you taking all these Uber rides into account? They're ex-pensive as hell." She catches the driver eyeing her in the rearview, and she smiles after her delivery.

The man nods in return.

"They do raise their rates," I say, and the driver full-on ignores me. "Any way and any time they want."

"I keep regretting being so harsh about our car. Maybe it was an asset. Shitty as it was, gas was the only expense. Two rides in these, and we've spent the same as we did on a full tank."

"It was a hazard though. I was sure to die on the road to El Harar."

"But I feel like the money that just came in is already in some-one else's hands."

"Fueling the economy and whatnot."

She doesn't laugh at this, rather shakes her head with pursed lips, "What I mean is, we need a financial plan. This isn't just pocket money for us to go spending around."

In front of us, the traffic loosens for an instant, and we inch forward, but it seems like our driver will miss the yellow traffic lights while texting on his phone.

"No, go for it; yellow here means go fast," I tell him, but he stops. The cars on the cross street invade our open lanes to glory.

The traffic starts building up behind us, and vendors soon swarm the lanes between cars, knocking on our windows to the tune of chicles, cacahuates, mazapán, even a blind man with veiny, all white eyes and a small recorder hanging from his neck singing "Cielito Lindo," adding a maraca-like swagger with a tin of coins. Just the sight of his eyes steals most of the air from my lungs.

On the navigation app's screen, our arrival time at the duplex has increased by four minutes.

"Fuck this," my wife says, looking into the rearview again. "Sir, we're getting off here, please. Swipe to complete the trip . . . Yes, thank you."

The fear of our daughter drifting into a floating position seems to have gone from her mind, and she's already jerking the handle of the door.

We exit into the hot smoke of exhaust, the buzz and tick of engines, and the rumble of a speeding Metrobús in its shielded lane.

She looks around in every direction, at the swirls of smog that have encircled us, like she's staring at the failure of all her work— this doomed city that can't be saved, that could never house her ecological utopias.

I hold her lower back and belly, as if our daughter could slip out. "You're sure this was wise?"

"I'd rather walk than be robbed." She nabs the phone from my hands and uninstalls my Uber app.

"Sure you want to do that? You can't afford all this stress."

I lead her forward against the heavy flow of cargo trucks blowing out black smoke, the smell of dog shit so pungent it makes me check my shoes to make sure I didn't step on a turd somewhere, the turds the Famous-Armless-Writer grapples with on a daily basis.

"Walking is good too. She can use a walk," she says.

While I nod, the smell of burnt gasoline becomes so sharp that I hack up some deep phlegm from my throat and spit it out to see my bloody snot splattered over the pavement.

"Classy," my wife says, "I see it's not just your eye that's bloody."

"This city, not quite the ideal place for me," but then I quiet when we come to a point where the sidewalk thins and then vanishes. Expressways lead in various directions, overhead and down below, cars zipping to the right and left, the city's roar always on the rise, a touch louder than one can take.

"Is this really where we want her to grow up?" my wife asks, a firm hand on her belly.

32

Prepped for my surgery, lying belly-up on the gurney, I'm already imagining the clear white of my bad eye—a white as clear as the space between the stanzas of my poems, the pure backdrop of an empty page.

33

But as I'm wheeled down a long corridor, staring up at the endless stream of glaring, white lights or to the sides at the everyday hospital vignettes, all I see are people with ugly illnesses, none of which can get an alleged quick fix like mine.

My eye surgeon, the red-haired ophthalmologist's associate, walks alongside my gurney, hand on my forearm, already dressed in navy blue scrubs, hairnet, and face mask, her eyes—uncanny, gray eyes with marble-like whites and pupils the deep black of an obsidian stone—are vibrant on the only bit of skin left uncovered. Eyes both feline and beautiful.

"I can't wait to have eyes like yours."

She laughs knowingly, perhaps suggesting that the ordinary civilian can never attain the eyes of an ophthalmologist—a god versus a mortal sort of condescension.

"At least I won't have the eye of the undead anymore," a note that earns me a more earnest laugh.

"A week following the surgery, you'll have to come back to see if it hasn't resurfaced. If it *has*, it's a very simple procedure."

"Wait, what?"

"And you'll have to wear a patch for a while. Even the smallest trace of a sunbeam can bring the pterygium right back."

"But she said it would be gone for good. That's what she told me, your partner."

"Oh, did she now? No, that's not right. That's a myth."

"A myth?"

She gives me a subtle smile, "Sure, the myth of pterygium."

"Sounds like a Greek tragedy in the making."

She laughs again, full-on this time. "Look, most likely, it will be gone and not come back. We're the best at it, rest assured."

"Best at removing pterygiums?"

She stoops forward and stares at me wide-eyed. "Look at these eyes," she says, smugly, but the up-close, kaleidoscopic sight of them, the retreating gray of her irises, catching glints of blue and green, is enough for me to take her word for it.

They wheel me along, and someone tosses a sheet of paper onto the gurney.

"You'll have to sign that. Just a consent form for going under full anesthesia."

"*Full anesthesia*? I didn't know I was going fully under."

"What exactly *did* you think?"

"Local, I guess, half a buzz."

"You want me cutting at your eye while you're half awake?" she asks, miming a scissoring motion with her fingers. "I can't imagine such a nightmare."

"When you put it that way," I say, getting a sudden flash of my mercurial daughter on that ultrasound screen, then a future flash of her, a grown, nameless girl, running about a grassy field. "People can die under anesthesia, can't they?"

She flicks my arm, "Come on, zero something percent. You could have died on your way over here. There are higher chances of that."

"I was hoping you'd say that was a myth too."

She clears her throat. "No. It happens. But it won't happen to you."

Shutting my eyes, I plunge into the recollection of coffee and rice over the symmetric patterns of the Persian rug at El Harar.

"No. I won't go under. Get me out of this thing. Take me back."

"You're in the best of hands."

"No, sorry, this isn't up for a coin toss."

On that, the surgeon flips open a cosmetic mirror in front of my face. "See that?" She brings it close to my face—the inner side of my right eye is a deep burgundy red, the creamy tissue flooding over the boundary of my cornea.

I move her hand away. "No, I have a child on the way. I can't." I tear the consent form in half.

"You're making a scene."

"I don't care," I say, ripping the consent form into more pieces.

"OK, then," the surgeon holds the gurney until the men pushing it stop. Turning to them, she says, "For those of you who thought the crazy shit came *after* the anesthesia."

They chuckle while she peels the latex gloves off her hands and tosses them over me.

Walking away behind me, her footsteps clatter and recede. The men turn me around and start pushing the gurney in the direction we came from.

Watching the consent form's pieces slipping off and fluttering away behind us, I settle into an oncoming slumber, as if they had, indeed, pumped their chemicals in me, the prospect of a white eye blurring, waning into the past.

34

The Would-Be-Writer pays me a juicy advance for his book project without any notice—his way of committing me to it long-term. The payment comes with the stipulation that my presence is required at an independent public library reading only a few blocks from our duplex, featuring the Famous-Armless-Writer and an American author I've never heard of before. After squirting some eye drops on my pterygium and leaving my wife cutting up more and more paper trees for her mock-up, I set off and find the Would-Be-Writer smoking a cigarette outside the library, dressed in all black, wearing a pretentious trench coat that seems unnecessary in this warm weather and that falls like a cape all the way to the dusty ground. When he spots me, he tosses his cigarette into a flower pot and offers me his weak handshake. "You made it after all."

"You made it sound like a requirement."

He brushes off my words and starts in the direction of the glass door of the library, out of which dashes one of the Famous-Armless-Writer's mutts, his black and white coat boasting a metallic sheen. The Would-Be-Writer whistles the dog over, but it ignores him and lifts its leg, shooting a stream of piss against a brick wall before sprinting back in.

We follow the dog's path into the packed event, where the Would-Be-Writer seems as poised as ever despite what he and I both know: he is not the writer he wants to be, and tonight, he is wrapped in a shroud of artificial self-confidence. Leading me around with his quick stride, he runs down a gauntlet of names and faces that delete themselves from my head the second I'm introduced to them, leaving only a blur of spectacles I suspect are fake, of fedoras tipped over tinted scalps, of self-drawn tattoos promising old-age regret. It's like walking into a costume party themed around the symbolist greats, packed with attendants who could well be the Halloween avatars of Mallarmé and Apollinaire, with their hats and bulging eyes, their thick beards and bushy moustaches. Every time I'm required to shake a hand or kiss a cheek, I try positioning myself at a calculated diagonal, offering only my left profile in hopes of hiding my pterygium.

Once we slice through the crowd, we head towards the far end of the windowless library, thick with beer breath and human heat, where we meet the American writer who will be reading alongside the Famous-Armless-Writer. The man, whose rich tawny skin glows under the white lights of the library, stands stiff next to the podium, intoed, a beer caught in his hands which meet at genital height, fig-leafed like a Greek statue. He only changes his posture in response to the Would-Be-Writer's imminent onslaught, who, in an attempt at making a good impression, extends both his arms in greeting. "Hola, Estridentista," he tells the man once he has him trapped in a hug, adding a gentle pat on his back. The Would-Be-Writer looks Lilliputian within the American's embrace—a tall, outlandishly handsome man with clear, honey-tinged eyes.

I shake his hand, which is cold and wet from his sweaty beer, once the Would-Be-Writer lets go of him. "So, you're a Stridentist? I thought those were unique to *this* country."

He cocks his head and grins, and the Would-Be-Writer seems to widen his eyes in surprise.

"Solo soy una poeta," the American-Faux-Stridentist says, clearly referring to himself in the feminine indefinite article despite what I had at first taken to be an overwhelmingly masculine appearance. Is there more to be read between the lines here? Are there traits there that point to an understated gender fluidity? It seems unlikely—he's surely just another Gringo Mexicophile, one of the many, seeking the *exotic* down here, all of whom believe they can immediately master Spanish by subtly morphing English words into Spanish and thus negate their all too evident *gringo-ness*—and so I probe:

"*Una* poeta?" I ask, with stark emphasis, but the Would-Be-Writer flicks my elbow and smiles, showing too many of his teeth.

"Sí, sí," the American-Faux-Stridentist says, "de Michigan, Norte."

I stare at him with raised brows, and the Would-Be-Writer's laugh beside me is whinnying, almost desperate. "He's on board too," he says, nodding my way and then slapping my back with more force than I would like. "The book, he'll be editing the book," he pauses and clears his throat. "Awkward as he is, he sure has a clinical eye."

While the American-Faux-Stridentist has a swig of his beer, I blush at the Would-Be-Writer's comment, wondering whether the jab was a calculated allusion to my pterygium or if it was more of a case of fortuitous wit. Whatever it was, it lays me off the man's Spanish and makes me think of how I could've had clear eyes by now if I hadn't chickened out. The American-Faux-Stridentist has another long gulp from his beer, and before the conversation takes the dreaded turn to my eye, I point to his bottle. "Where can I get one of those?"

"Sí," he says, nodding sideways towards a red bucket on the floor filled with ice melting over beer bottles.

"Can you get me a cold one?" the Would-Be-Writer says, and I head over and kneel in front of the bucket. As I'm excavating two bottles of Modelo Especial from a layer of ice, one of the Famous-Armless-Writer's dogs approaches me and sniffs my arm. I shove it away and get some angry but silent stares, then bring the beers over to the Would-Be-Writer, who has taken a seat in the middle of the crowd.

I look around for an opener, but there is none to be found. The American-Faux-Stridentist notices and uncaps our beers with his molars, a hiss escaping the bottle as he bites and tugs. He then spits the caps back out, and they *tink* to the ground. I thank him by clinking our bottles, to which he responds with a wink of an eye.

Finally, the Famous-Armless-Writer materializes from the bathroom, followed by a flushing sound. He heads for the table at the front, his two dogs following him, agile, veering around people and chairs. He sits in the middle of the table, soon flanked by the American-Faux-Stridentist, who rubs the inside of his mouth with his thumb, as if to soothe the pain in his gums after biting open our two beers. I take the seat the Would-Be-Writer is saving for me.

The room full, the whole audience equipped with drinks, a

loud, scratchy tapping of the microphone signals the start of the reading, and, in the rush of people taking their seats, I get a twitch in my right eye. I bend my upper body, facing down, head between my legs, then rub my eye while uncapping my eye drops. I tilt my head and place the bottle next to my eyelids to allow a few drops to slide in. I leave my head as it is, hoping the drops can have their full effect, staring down at chair legs, empty beer bottles, and the dogs among the dusty shoes.

I raise my head when the American-Faux-Stridentist is introduced and the Would-Be-Writer tugs on my sleeve.

A useless list of his prior publications is read by the library's director, a thin, balding man, who has clearly put a lot of effort into evenly combing the few hairs he has left over the shimmering north pole of his head. His voice runs deep out of the speakers, which are placed behind us, near the library's front door. Looking at him, I can't help but notice a striking resemblance to someone, who exactly, I don't know.

When the American-Faux-Stridentist is handed the microphone, he attempts an introduction to his work in Spanish, again studded with mistakes and odd around the edges; his misuse of tenses creates the sense of a mind-bending time warp.

From what I can make out, he'll be reading from a long poem originally written by a British poet in the 1960s, which he has translated into Spanish, a poem that, *incidentally*, was a great source of inspiration for the writings of the Famous-Armless-Writer, who, sitting at his side, nods in appreciation, followed by a piercing bark by one of his dogs.

A few chuckles spark throughout the crowd, and the American-Faux-Stridentist switches to English for his reading. It's a rather moving long prose poem, subtly laced with black humor, about a tree that was struck by lightning and deprived of its largest branch and everything that lived in it from squirrels, snakes, birds, moss, worms, microbes, all of them experiencing not only loss but change, transmutation as it were, and above all, adaptation. Beside me, the Would-Be-Writer nods along while the American-Faux-Stridentist's words fill the room with true grace, adding beautiful ups and downs to his voice, sardonic pauses, making for a tranquilizing effect that is directly opposed to what he accomplished while speaking in Spanish.

When the poem comes to an end, the Would-Be-Writer offers a standing ovation, which irks a few people sitting behind him and reduces the rest of the applause to the sound of the tail end of a rain stick.

The Famous-Armless-Writer stoops over the microphone, cutting off the man reading the bios and publication credits whose face, I can now tell, looks like the picture of Homero Aridjis on the back of my wife's book.

"I'll begin with this brief passage," the Famous-Armless-Writer says, his dogs now sitting beside him like statues, and immediately plunges into a second-person narrative about his lost arm, one that recedes into a soliloquy of sorts, and as the words grow louder, the dogs dash into the crowd again, zigzagging between the chairs and brushing against our legs. The Would-Be-Writer picks one of the dogs up and holds it in his lap, his coat immediately gathering the dog's shedding fur. The Would-Be-Writer listens to the reading with an expression that I read as terror, perhaps just now realizing he must match the quality of the Famous-Armless-Writer's words for his book not to be doomed. As he listens, he bites his lip and stares intently ahead, burying his face in the dog's fur, which makes me gag a little. I find myself surprised that I'm not as disgusted by the proximity of the dog and its smell of an old man's sweater as I would normally be, captured instead by the final words rocking from the Famous-Armless-Writer's throat; the final sentences are a dual reckoning, as if spoken by the lost arm itself, then by him, armless. The final stanza lingers—*Where? I still feel you*—words that could well be spoken by that previous tree or any of the poem's animate and inanimate characters. The idea of these writers collaborating on a book begins to gather motion in my thoughts, but where does the story of the Would-Be-Writer's stillborn twin fit in again?

A short silence follows. Then the Famous-Armless-Writer folds the book shut and we are drowned in applause. The Would-Be-Writer lets go of the dog, which leaps from his legs towards his master, and offers yet another standing ovation, but he is not the only one this time. The dog hair showers down from his coat to the floor with every clap of his hands.

The Famous-Armless-Writer is immediately mobbed by the crowd, which moves up to him like high tide, the Would-Be-Writer included, and so I take the last of my tepid beer outside and gulp it down under the feeble streetlight. The whir of electricity cables hums as I watch the gradual outpour of the audience. Above the library, the night blackens with the porous texture of volcanic rock, and the last people to exit are the Would-Be-Writer alongside the two readers and the two dogs—a fetid smell clear in the air as they come near me. He formally introduces me to the Famous-Armless-Writer, telling him I will be editing the upcoming book, and I can tell that he vaguely recognizes my face as he shakes my hand.

"What happened to your eye?" he asks me, the fetid smell stronger, coming from his mouth.

"Pollution," I say, looking up at the haze around streetlights. "This city, not quite the ideal place for me."

He nods and winces, as if searching for some meaning in my words, "You should do something about it. While you still can."

"Yeah, no, that's the plan," I say, trying to hold my eyesight on his.

"So, are you coming with? The whole literary team is here," the Would-Be-Writer tells me, crouching to pet both dogs at once.

"No, my pregnant wife awaits me."

"Seguro? Killer party you'll be missing," the American-Faux-Stridentist says. "Already savoring the pulque and the mezcal, me."

I shake my head.

"Well," the Famous-Armless-Writer says, "good to finally meet you. See you around," and he offers me the shake of his hook this time, which extends its iciness down my limbs. Grinning, he adds, "Hope you liked the reading."

"Loved it," I say, glad to let go of the hook.

The American-Faux-Stridentist offers me his rehearsed Mexican handshake and quick hug, which, to his credit, he has mastered, and the Would-Be-Writer offers nothing more than an awkward fist bump. They walk away under the feeble light, the dogs in a light jog in front of them. The thickness of that awful smell they brought follows them and ultimately vanishes with them behind the corner.

After finishing my now flat beer with a long gulp and placing the empty bottle beside the library's door, my phone pings and shows a text message by the Would-Be-Writer:

hope you're deep into my pages already. brought you here tonight so you could see the quality it must match.

In a flood of rage, I turn off my phone and walk home down an empty Marsella Street.

Back in the duplex, my wife is lying flat on the couch, miniature paper trees balanced over her stout belly. "Love it," she says. "Guns by day, words by night."

"If only the words were mine."

"Come on. No pouting." She balances another paper tree on her belly. Unable to avoid a smirk, she says, "So, how is your very own Verlaine doing?"

"Very funny. If he could only write like Verlaine."

"That bad, eh?"

I nod and walk closer to her, watching the miniature jungle she has planted over the hill that houses our daughter, "Those trees, there seems to be more and more of them."

"The city needs them. Our daughter will too."

I fall heavily on the couch and the trees crumble to the floor.

"Ooh!" she says, her mouth and eyes forcibly open wide. "Bad omen."

"Is there any other kind?" I say, resting my head on both her and our daughter.

35

Ferocious traffic clogs the streets. At every Metrobús station, crowds thickly accumulate, and four buses come by and leave before we can get to the front of the line.

My wife's newest request is that we take public transportation to our pediatrician. According to her urbanism formulas, if one-fourth of single-car drivers were to switch to either the Metrobús or the subway, the pollution hanging above us and oozing into us with our every breath would dissolve from "health risk factor to nuisance," these final words delivered with a knowing nod and a raised index finger.

Stretching my right eye open for her to peer into, I ask, "Is this a health risk or nuisance?" She finds this hilarious.

The sweltering air at the Hamburgo Metrobús station is sooty and vaporous; my skin seeps grease-thick sweat, and it feels like the hiss of the approaching bus might bring about some comfort, but the sight of black smoke puffing from the rear muffler as it arrives has my wife vehemently shaking her head.

It's a battle to get in, with my wife holding on to my T-shirt and then leading me all the way to the back.

"Is all this from the pollution?" I say, rubbing the thin film of dust that has gathered against the window.

She nods, her lips pursed, then a mild, disapproving shake of the head. "Can you even believe these busses are not electric?"

"Welcome to the third world, chock full of rich men making billions in the oil trade."

"Yeah, well, I hope they die a long and cruel death from emphysema."

Her ire is cut short as the bus jolts forward, shaking every passenger inside. Holding her by the forearm, I ask, "You're sure you want to be doing this as far along as you are? It's not like we're changing the city by taking this bus."

"What this city needs is a proactive example. Enough with progressive theory."

"How about you do it when you go back to work? After the baby is born."

She holds her thoughts, then finally nods, in resignation it seems, and I nod too, as if I'd won some sort of contest.

"But *you* should do it every time," she says, laying her stiff index finger on my chest.

I get the urge to roll my eyes, but all I do is nod, which makes her let go of the subject.

Inside the bus, stop by stop, the air thickens as more and more people come in, their smells, their holes, their flatulence, all yellowing the already filthy windows. When we finally reach our stop, my wife shoves me into the outpouring crowd. "Go for it. This is it," she says. And the stream of bodies spits us into another layer of the Mexico City commuter's dystopia—the vendors swarming the station, the food stalls on street corners with their burnt oil fumes.

From the pedestrian bridge that leads to the pediatrician's office, the view is ochre-grim. Cars zip by underneath us, and the buildings afar are shrouded in the thickening smog, its sick breeze burning into my eye.

I wince and rub.

"Everything OK?" my wife asks.

"No." I keep on rubbing the ever-increasing pain.

36

"Did you walk here?" the pediatrician asks as we enter his office, one eye fully open, the other squeezed to a slit.

My wife says no and I nod, but he isn't really looking or listening, rather guides us to the ultrasound, where we find that our daughter is still in a sitting position, snug, her head towards the upper part of the uterus.

"She still hasn't flipped," the pediatrician says. "I was hoping she had."

My wife shuts her eyes and attempts a loud, soothing breath.

"So, what do we do?" I ask.

"We give her a few more weeks. If she still doesn't turn, we'll have to do something about it."

Nodding, I can feel more sweat dripping down my face and puddling under my clothes.

"And do something about your eye too," he says. "No point in waiting with that one."

I walk over to my wife to cut him off; I kiss her warm forehead. The pediatrician opens up a drawer and pulls out a blood pressure gauge. He ties its band around her arm and squeezes a plastic valve.

"We have to keep those stress levels down," he says. "She won't flip if we don't." Turning to me, he adds, "You know how to use these?" He points to the band tied around my wife's arm and squeezes the valve once more. "You'll have to do it every morning and every night. Make sure her blood pressure is steady."

He removes the band from my wife's arm and tosses the snaky thing my way.

37

The final day before starting work at El Harar has me stuck in a neoliberal café of polished wood and marble surfaces, downing foamy doppios with the Would-Be-Writer. The LED lights above us are white, garish—reminiscent of the days when the sun shone through the clouds. Under the hum of slow electronic music, I slouch and wince as I go over his newest draft, my obscured eye moving quickly over prose heavy with exposition and stilted dialogue, suggestions of removals he steadfastly ignores. I find myself doodling on a separate sheet of paper while I read, as if my mind were asleep. His mumbling beside me, though, faintly returns me to a present semi-lucidity, "This'll be a very relevant book . . . "

I feign a nod as my yellow highlighter expands over the white of his pages, swift and sure, marking the pages with a bone-tickling sound.

Seeing that his words have no effect on me, he keeps on mumbling to himself, "I'm glad I could tie all this together to the others' work, writing through my voice and my brother's, connecting it to the story of that tree and its innards and the story of the lost arm."

I give him a mild shrug, resisting the urge to tell him that perhaps it might be best to get his own voice right first, forget about his brother's, or that he shouldn't trick the reader, making us believe, at first, that his brother, this ghostly presence in the text, was at some point alive.

In his story, the unborn twin—referred to at times as *the shadow* or *the better half*—appears out of the blue, an omnipresence of sorts. The action is narrated in the present tense, making for an odd time warp throughout the rest of the story, which is narrated in the past tense, shifting between first- and third-person singular. It's only in the second to last chapter that our Would-Be-Writer reveals his brother was already dead at the moment of birth and that he is "channeling" his voice, perhaps the voice of his unconscious. A symbolist would say this absence might be a stand-in for purity, which makes me feel like the intent of the text might be on point; it's only the style, the timeline, and the structural know-how that have gone terribly amiss. To prove my point, I try recommending him a few creation myths to help him understand the benefits of a linear narrative, of beginning at an actual beginning. I also ramble on about the overall structure of the Greek tragedy, where the utter sense of loss is redeemed by paradox and, even perhaps, a key moralist message.

"Take a good look at *Oedipus, Icarus, Antigone*," I shrug. "There are so many to pick from."

He nods, pinching his chin.

"The reader would benefit from a prologue here. The rise from mimesis to catharsis—take advantage of your own personal tragedy."

He keeps on nodding while sipping his doppio and wiping the foam from his upper lip with a canine lap of the tongue.

As the glare inside the café becomes unbearable, I fear my pterygium might have grown during our meeting. I have to shut my eyes and press on my eyelids before carrying on with his final paragraphs, the words on the page shifting, wobbling, coming together, and overlapping.

When I'm done, I cap the highlighter and arrange the bulk of his manuscript into place, tapping its sides to fully align every rebellious page.

Looking up at him, I see a denser cloudiness in my right eye. Bright scintillas float madly around my vision, and the swaths of intense light are blurred. For a second, it's hard to distinguish things from each other, their full definition, as everything is bending away from its conventional shape.

So? he says, verdict.

Look over the notes, *closely,* I say, handing him the manuscript.

He takes the pages from me, doubtful.

Get me a new draft by next weekend, I say. Make it as different as you possibly can.

He clicks his tongue and says, I was hoping we were done here. We have to go to print soon. There are deadlines to be met.

I breathe out and rub my bad eye, hard. Faint, cloudy images travel across the frame of my sight. Go on. Go make the chair bleed, I tell him. The only way is through.

Nodding, he packs the manuscript into his bag, shakes my hand, and gives me a light hug before heading for the pale light outside.

Forgetting something? I call out.

He turns, blushing. Oh, *that*, right, he says, and slips me my payment.

And extra hours?

He slips me another hundred.

After finishing my third doppio, I pack my things and head for the bathroom. Staring closely at the mirror, I find that my pterygium has indeed gained more territory; it's well over my iris now, pupil-hungry. My sight alternately focuses and blurs as I cover and uncover my bad eye with my hand.

Outside, there is not a trace of blue in the sky. Walking under an invisible sun lost behind the haze, I get a text from my mother, which I read covering my bad eye, *You start tomorrow, do not forget,* and it's like I can hear her pernicious tone, a clear voice, at last, which makes the sight of rice and coffee beans leap back to me, their portent, the stories of stillborn children loud in the voice inside my head.

38

Our duplex greets me with the smell of habanero and pork skin, and I can hear the shuffling of my wife's feet on the upper floor.

In the middle of our living room, her drafting table boasts the complex design of her ecological utopia, and I have to really lean in to look at it in detail. Paper trees populate the mock-up, a green corridor running down what would be Reforma, from Chapultepec up until Bucareli. There are no cars on the famed avenue, only trees, tens of them arching over pins that surely symbolize pedestrians. The Metrobús line runs on either side of the street, but it has become something more akin to a tram, a carousel, endless cabins on either direction.

This is really something, I yell up.

Her footsteps bang slowly and heavily down the stairs. Like it? she asks, and I can see a certain gloom in her face, the lower lips of her eyes irritated red.

Everything OK?

She can barely make herself nod.

Turning to face the mock-up, I run a hand over the tiny trees. So many of them, I say. What if they're to no avail?

All we can do is try, hope for the best. She runs her hand along her trees until it meets mine, placing the knot of our fingers over her belly and sinking her chin in the hollow of my shoulder.

We look out the window at the gray sky with its darkening spots, at the rumbling of a cargo truck on the street expelling more black smoke, at everything on Marsella Street drifting out of shape.

39

Nothing at first. Then a wet wind followed by the darkening imprint of rain dots on the gravel: these timid drizzles that bathe the outskirts of the city, never reaching our great, polluted valley itself. The purity of it, the clean air striking cool against my eyes, doesn't help. My pterygium is still there, the sight ahead of me blurry, dreamlike. In the distance, like a grainy film, my mother opens the stainless steel trunk at the entrance of El Harar's shooting range, searches inside, and pulls out a silver-plated gun with a leather grip.

The first sound, one that pierces the suburban quiet, is the blast from her personalized .45 caliber. Her bullet leaves a hole in the black wooden figure that is shaped like a person at the far end of the property.

I feel the air grow colder in my chest, as if the bullet had gone through me, and say, Ever thought this is what might bring death to this family, one of these guns?

My mother belts out a laugh, malevolent, it seems at first, but probably just intended to be sarcastic.

Ah, the nervous words of the apprentice, my brother says, stepping up to the shooting range too; his strides are long and loud over the shifting gravel. Standing next to my mother, he slips on shooting glasses with bright red lenses. Stretching his arms forward like my mother did, he holds a 9-millimeter straight, aimed at the wooden shadow ahead, then fires, once, twice, then empties the cartridge. His hands jerk back with every pull of the trigger. The bullets land—even though they seem to only appear—scattered over the human silhouette: head, arms, some of them out of target.

Alex, Alex, my mother chides him. You still lack the poise, the cold-blooded shot.

My brother laughs, his own version of malevolence, and my mother turns to me before I can avert my eyes. From the trunk beside her, she pulls out something that can only be described as a war rifle and places it on a mound of dirt that bears some resemblance to the shape of my wife's pregnant belly. The weapon shimmers, catching occasional glints of pale daylight. A belt of high-range bullets is attached to it and coiled beside it.

Go on now, she says. Initiation.

I shake my head looking down at the gravel, at a single file of ants diligently carrying food for their queen. No chance.

You want that job, that paycheck, you fire every bullet on that belt, she says, pointing backward in the general direction of the wounded shadow.

I stand my ground, stare straight into her eyes.

I'm serious, she says, then pulls me by the elbow and shoves me in the direction of the rifle.

My steps are cumbersome, and my brother indulges in an exaggerated smirk. Reaching the mound, I turn back to look at them both, my brother still grinning and my mother giving me a double nod.

Hesitantly, I kneel on the gravel, wondering how to position myself over the weapon, veering around the coiled bullet belt to the sound of more of my brother's laughter. I turn to them again.

My mother is grinning now too, her yellowing teeth a stain across her face.

How do you even shoot this fucking thing?

This *fucking thing* is one of the finest assault rifles known to man, my mother replies, folding her arms. Crouch all the way to the ground. Lay next to it. Make love to it.

My brother takes out his phone and holds it horizontally in my direction.

Cut that shit out, I tell him, but his hands keep steady.

Go on, my mother says. Figure it out, and so I lay adjacent to the thing, holding its cold, wet metal, the gravel pricking my legs and arms, parts of my ribcage.

There we go, my mother says when I'm lying like soldiers do, gripping the rifle with both hands, its back end stiff against my shoulder. The rain continues to fall with a steadier patter, gnawing languidly at my body. Come on now, her words cut through the murmurs of the rain. We're getting wet here. We don't have all day.

Facing the wooden target ahead, I look into the rifle's crosshairs with my good eye, focusing my sight on the human-shaped shadow before the wall.

I breathe in. The trigger is light, the blasts not as piercing and loud.

After the first four bullet shells drop from the rifle, there are no marks on the shadowy man at the end of sight, which my brother finds hilarious. When I turn to them, he is still filming me, and my mother does a rolling gesture with her hand.

The whole belt, she says, the rain now weighing her hair down, raindrops rendered as transparent marks on her white shirt. We're not leaving until you fire every bullet.

My breath out is hoarse, my sight clear through the crosshairs. I listen to the downpour before pulling the trigger. The gentlest of squeezes has the rifle smashing against my shoulder, a swath of time that seems soundless, bullet shells gathering on the ground, quickly accumulating, bullet holes on the human silhouette, appearing all over it, blasts bouncing off the adobe walls of El Harar.

Then the trigger resists the squeeze of my finger. The belt that held the bullets has slid through the rifle, coming out empty on the other end.

The first sound I register after I'm done is the patter of the rain muffling my mother's clapping.

All done. You can go tend to your paperwork now, she says. Your brother will bring you up to speed.

I turn and lay faceup on the gravel, watching them walk to the house, growing smaller in the distance, the rain blurring the landscape, falling over every inch of my skin, bursting on my face, breaking over the metallic surface of the rifle.

Fully soaked, I allow some time for my limbs to stop shaking. Then I walk to the house too, straight to the bathroom to dry myself off, where, standing in front of the mirror, I look at my reflection through my eyesight's new haze. My pterygium has spread over most of the green of my eye, a meaty branch reaching for the first trace of pupil, robbing everything around me of its sharp edges. Winking doesn't help focus my vision either, rather it lends an eerie, dim white over everything around me.

40

Again, I wink and empty yet more drops into my eye, realizing I'll soon be finished with the bottle. Everything in front of me remains behind this blurry definition.

Back at my desk, I find the screen of my phone illuminated, showing a message from my wife, which I read covering my bad eye:

LOL, Arthur, I just saw you shooting some rounds! capped with the guffawing emoji.

Fucking Alex, I mumble to myself, then pick up the phone to respond:

I believe I am in hell, therefore I am.

The light shot from the screen is white, glaring, a touch brighter than I can take.

41

My wife's new pregnancy-related insomnia has us both working late into the night, each of us under the warm light of a desk lamp and the weak streaks of streetlight seeping in through the window's impurities. She writes on a long paper roll, spread out over the length of her drafting table, trying to work out an equation which includes not only the number of trees endemic to the Tenochtitlán Valley needed to clean the polluted air in the stretch of the city represented in her mock-up—Reforma between Chapultepec and Bucareli—but also the amperage and number of solar panels needed to feed her carousel of public transportation. Her calculations have her, more than anything, slicing up more trees with her cutter and inching them closer together in what rapidly becomes a green cluster more akin to a green jungle not yet tainted. She cuts, slices, folds, and binds.

People in this city, they used to talk fútbol and telenovelas, she says, about every bit of hearsay around the neighborhood. Now all they do is talk about the pain in their eyes and in their throats, how many goddamn pollutants are hanging in the air.

Tell me about it, I say, and return to my task at hand, which is certainly of a lesser complexity but still difficult due to the ever-expanding leak on my computer screen and the blur in my eye. The editing consists—in the slim swath of screen still allowing the document's visibility—of adding nouns, predicates, verbs, commas, and full stops when they are needed, stressing the necessity of definite articles for the sake of assertive writing, then rewriting sentences so they gain a quality worthy of going to print under the same name as the Famous-Armless-Writer and the American-Faux-Stridentist. There's also the removal of full paragraphs, cutting and pasting them elsewhere so that they form a linear narrative, the words *forget you ever wrote this* in eye-vein-red text.

When I run out of patience, I flip to the Famous-Armless-Writer's section, and I have to really nitpick, adding commas, word suggestions to sentences that don't really need perking up, hoping he can understand my democratizing gesture.

His text for the book will mirror the Would-Be-Writer's and the translated poem of the tree. It tells the story of the development of his relationship with his late wife, who on their first dates would hold the phantom of his right hand as they walked down the street, would kiss the phantom of his right hand during intercourse, and would later hold the hook he has for a hand, would allow its icy grip on her breasts during moments of intimacy.

Bathed by the light of her lamp, my wife cuts, slices, and binds; her profile, silhouetted by the warm light, is slim atop and bulging at the middle. It's a sight poetic enough to make me walk to her, run my hand across her back, down her arms, over our daughter inside her smooth belly.

She turns to face me, kisses my cheek, then peers at my right eye.

Arthur, she says, her eyebrows raised at a worrisome slant. That eye, it's starting to scare me.

I rest my chin on her forehead and say, I sometimes wish it wasn't there anymore.

She grabs my face and holds it in front of hers with both her hands, then covers my bad eye with one, lending me a more focused view of her face.

There, she says, and kisses the hand she placed over my eye.

42

The few hours of sleep have given me two bloodshot eyes that somewhat camouflage my pterygium—as if I was just living through the ravages of a drunken stint.

Outside our building, the air is dead-still, and a sulfur tang lives in it; the buzz of traffic is clear and distinct all around me. Crossing the street and scampering in my direction are the Famous-Armless-Writer's dogs. They circle me, sniff my legs, and flap their tails against my ankles. I kick them away and begin my walk towards the nearest Metrobús station. The Famous-Armless-Writer is nowhere in sight though, and his dogs begin following me. I try to scare them away without success, and it takes the harmless toss of a street pebble in their direction to get them dashing off in the opposite way.

My Metrobús ride is as hellish as last time, my body hemmed in on all sides, the windows streaked with rinse marks—even if there's not much to see through the glass, just gray clouds of smog and dust breaking slowly over the bus as I rumble to my next stop. The man beside me is reading *El Metro*, its cover page framing fallen corpses and pools of blood underneath them. I cover my right eye to read the headline SLAUGHTERED FOR FUN in ink as red as the blood and the subtitle, 14 SHOT TO DEATH AT A PARTY WITH HIGH CALIBER AUTOMATIC WEAPONS.

The assault rifle I fired immediately comes to mind. The bullets smashing against the target and the walls of El Harar. But the bus stops and heaves before I can read further.

I get out where my brother asked me to, right on his way to El Harar, and purchase my own copy of *El Metro* while I wait, reading deep into the story with a clenched eye, skimming for a line about the weapons, the brand, the caliber, which the article notes is of a strength that only the country's armed forces are known to legally possess, and how El Cártel de Jalisco Nueva Generación claims responsibility for the actions. Turning the page, I hear a blaring honk: the polished glimmer of my brother's Audi A6 stops before me, creating his own traffic jam, leading to angrier honks and lifted middle fingers behind the wobbling images of windshields.

I thought you were a man of poetry, he says when I sit down next to him, newspaper in hand, which I toss into his lap.

Murdered with high-caliber weapons.

Yeah, so?

Might it be one of *our* weapons, Alex?

Oh, I see. Is this about guilt, the whole *holier than thou* bit?

Do you care at all?

Look, maybe it would be better if you thought of yourself as a kitchen knife salesman.

Are you fucking serious?

You are selling commodities; you are not responsible for their use.

And what is the alternate use of an assault rifle? Killing your food? I didn't take you to be a game hunter.

You won't last the day with that outlook, big brother. Maybe you should keep to your poems.

And maybe you should realize the country you live in.

He sniffs and looks at the road ahead, Have it your way, then.

We sail towards El Harar, the silence now deep as we enter the highway lined with as many trees as my wife dreams of for her utopias. On my phone, there is a text from her:

Good luck within the walls of El Harar.

True life is elsewhere, I respond, next to the cockeyed emoji.

43

That night, we turn on the evening news, and I measure my wife's blood pressure. There seems to be no reason for alarm, and the piece of equipment assures the temporary health of our daughter, who is apparently satisfied to just go on sitting inside the womb forever.

The news begins with the daily update of murdered people since our government re-declared the war on drugs in 2006, the numbers now racing past a hundred thousand. Most of these people have been done in with bullets, the commodity I newly represent.

Yay, my wife says, level-voiced. More grind house shit. Who needs Tarantino when you have *México Lindo?* I say nothing and turn to her, widening my eyes as far as they go to fake outrage, as if by dealing arms, I could be in a position to be insulted.

Then they run the story I saw in the paper this morning with the newest developments. After the bloodbath that saw fourteen people killed in a standoff, the military raided a local bar and sequestered eleven young men, some of the alleged perpetrators, but all have yet to be accounted for. The screen then shifts to an image of all the weapons that were secured at the scene: a collection that could well be the innards of my mother's shooting range trunk.

No, my wife says, not this shit before bed. Stress levels, remember? She snaps the TV off, and the last thing I see before the screen's blackout is the grip of a rifle engraved with our family insignia.

A cold feeling washes over me, and I'm sure I've lost the color from my face.

What's wrong? my wife asks.

No, nothing, my words thick. Yeah, no, let's go to bed. That glare from the TV is no good for my eye.

44

Once I settle into a real routine—one marked by timetables, commuting, and other mindless tasks—I begin to get a feeling of emptiness in my chest and to see life, even if through a veil, as *the farce everyone has to perform*, words I copy from my mental ruminations and paste into the text box of my WhatsApp conversation with my wife.

During my mother and brother's absence, due to what they labeled *a very important meeting in the city*, El Harar proffers a real sense of stillness. Their absence also allows me to edit the Would-Be-Writer's latest draft—a text that looks and reads, more and more, like something I wrote myself.

During my self-appointed lunch break, I go outside, dragging my mother's lounger with me and placing it on the gravel to stare at a sky covered by clouds. Beneath the murmur-like shudders of tree leaves, a narcocorrido struggles to play from what sounds like a cheap piece of audio equipment beyond El Harar's wall—*with an AK / and a bazooka, taking aim / blowing off the heads / of whoever gets in the way*—a tune somehow relaxing despite the violence of its lyrics.

My lunch consists of food my wife prepared: a vegan chicken sandwich plucked directly from her new pregnancy diet, filled with food that is meant to make my daughter somersault in the warm, gelatinous matter of the womb.

Chewing large mouthfuls, I turn to look at my former Ford Bronco in the yard, past the state of decrepitude we kept it in, now forgotten, left to perish like a shipwreck washed ashore.

With the last bit of sandwich shoved down my throat, I recover the Would-Be-Writer's manuscript from my desk and bring it outside, trusting my good eye to watch out for more edits.

When I'm down on the lounger again, I hear the loud bolt of the gates opening, its metallic clink—too soon for my mother and brother's return.

I pick up her lounger and the manuscript pages and run back inside, hoping they won't catch sight of me.

Returning the piece of furniture to what should be its permanent spot on the Persian rug, I walk back outside to greet them and feign innocence, wearing the tired face that comes from bureaucratic work, but instead, I instantly feel a weakness in my legs at the sight of a camouflaged, military pickup truck racing towards me, a wake of dust rising behind it, filled with five soldiers with helmets, glasses, bulletproof vests, and heavy weapons riding in the back. One more soldier stands on a metallic structure atop the vehicle, lending him a lethal vantage point, over which a long, thick caliber rifle is perched, its canon vaguely pointed in my direction.

My whole body goes cold when the pickup comes to a halt in front of me. One of the soldiers descends from the cabin, while all the others pay a close watch. This one doesn't wear a helmet, instead sports one of those caps most often associated with genocidal autocrats. He removes his sunglasses and extends a hand my way, which is dry, papery, with a knot of blue veins meeting in his wrist. Looking straight at his face, I'm shocked to find a mild trace of a pterygium in his left eye, and for a moment, a rush of adrenaline runs through me, an improbable moment of recognition, which he either doesn't respond to or doesn't find amusing.

Is your name Alex?

I shake my head, No, sir. No doubt, he can see sweat gathering on my forehead, the light shivering of my body.

What *is* your name?

Arthur, I stutter, while in the background, the narcocorrido rambles on.

He nods with a squint, doubtful. How are you related to Alex?

I tell him Alex is either my brother or my mother but that I can't help much, that I've only just started working here.

Prove it.

How?

He hesitates, then hands me a long sheet of paper filled with stamps and signatures, This, here, is a warrant.

The piece of paper flutters in the clutch of his hand. I look it over, but my lack of knowledge in the business, my blurry sight, and the anxiety I'm struggling through while having a rifle pointed at me lends no meaning to the bellicose words. I stare at him, swallow a thick wad of spit.

We're here to look at every piece of your weaponry, he says. Sales, invoices, ammo, everything better be accounted for. Those books better be in order.

While I nod nonstop, he explains that the latest mass shootings have been executed with high-caliber weapons that use a specific bullet and are rare for these groups to have access to, some of which only the Mexican militia and police forces are known to possess and only *we* are known to sell.

You see the problem we have here, he says. That means it's either *us* who are shedding the blood or you have found yourselves new clients. Diversification? Is that what they call it?

The cloudy scenery starts to spin around me and my semi-digested faux chicken sandwich rushes to my throat, but I manage to swallow back down.

Ever since that *Fast and Furious* bullshit up north, he adds, tracking weapons has been a real motherfucker. So, we're here to make sure you're in the clear, that you're not working behind our backs.

I'm about to open the front door, let them take whatever they need, but the admiral suddenly retreats back to the pickup truck.

He gets in and, sticking his head out from the window, says, We'll wait for Alex right here. Then pointing at me, And you, dear commoner, are going to sit right there until he gets here.

I'm on the verge of asking if I can run inside to get a chair.

Right there, he says, and the soldier above points his rifle at the gravel beneath my feet.

My arms upraised, I lower my body slowly, fold my legs, and sit on the prickly gravel, which feels as if I'd sat on coffee beans, bullets, grains of rice.

After a few bloodthirsty verses in the narcocorrido, the admiral sticks his head out the window again, whistling the tune.

That shit in your eye, he says, fucking pain in the ass, isn't it?

My first reaction is to slip on my sunglasses, but I only nod while holding my position, the mouth of that rifle gaping at me.

45

The following morning, it's all over the news. The recent carnage has clear connections to my family's guns, specifically the kind of rifle I fired under the rain's patter.

The sounds around me now are similar to that day, only the drizzle is confined to our bathroom where my wife is showering and the gun blasts are coming from the television—a sound bite from the bloody night in question.

Just as my wife stops the shower, my phone shifts and rumbles over my desk, the words *Private Number* glaring on the black screen. The voice on the other end inquires about my name.

Who's asking?

He says he's a journalist from the newspaper *Animal Político*.

What is it you want?

Information, about bullets, shells, the ones cited in the news.

Wrong number. I'm just a poet.

Poet dealing weapons, where have I heard that one before?

Look, I can't help you.

The last I hear before hanging up is that my name and number are listed as the ammunition representative on my mother's weapon company's website.

My wife steps out of the bathroom, steam rushing in my direction. One towel covers her stout body, and another is wrapped around her head. I toss the phone onto the desk.

Arthur? What's wrong? You've got that ghostly color on your face again.

This whole *Arthur* thing. I don't know how much I'm into it anymore.

46

Sitting on her lounger, her legs folded and her hair tied in a pony-
tail, my mother lays out how the gears of this business turn: the
federal government must approve of our operations and must also
approve of every consortium or private client purchasing our guns
and bullets—all of which must be properly licensed—including
the Mexican police forces and the Mexican militia. In order for
us to make a real profit, selling vast amounts of guns and ammo
to the Mexican army and the Mexican police forces, we must sell
everything at a 25 percent discount. The corruption-riddled system requires nods of approval from several high-ranking officials
within the government, the army, and the police force, as well as
a sign off by the Department of Treasury. On occasion, we also
have to deal with oppositional agitators—activists, rival party lob-
byists, journalists, delinquent groups—depending on how rattled
the sociopolitical arena is at any given time. Now, the country
cannot forgo its heritage: We Mexicans adore our guns. We share
a history of violence all the way from conquest to independence,
passing along through the Christian War, the Revolution, the in-
surgence of the Zapatistas in Chiapas, and a forty-year drug war,
all that without taking into account our beloved crimes of passion,
the bullets fired after every adulterous kiss, after every betrayal,
after every tequila-emboldened contest of pride. Firing weapons,
we love. If one keeps quiet in the Mexican province, wherever
that may be, the gun blast is as common as the chirp of a bird or
the whir of the cicada. To avoid the ill-humored tantrums of all
that clockwork, my mother explains, it is sometimes necessary to
come bearing gifts. It's essential to keep everyone happy. Sure,
our weapons sometimes trickle down into the black market: once
they cross El Harar's walls, there's no telling where they'll end
up. The visit I was paid by the military is as common as it was
unannounced and was probably in response to the stain the recent
news brought to their impeccable institution. If a rifle was pointed
at me, it was, surely, only meant as an *incentive*, which as we well
know, in this country, is a synonym for *threat*. Either clear things
up or make it up to me—probably the latter, as the harm in the
public eye has already been done.

Cutting my mother's rambling short, my brother comes into the room, sharply dressed in a black suit; his steps are a loud tap, then noiseless over the rug. He nods in the direction of my mother, and she nods back.

So, off you go, she tells me. You're getting in the car with your brother and delivering the package hidden in its trunk to the secretary of defense.

Wait, no.

Slowly, she says, You're getting in the car with him. You have to be a recognizable face if you're going to deal with these people. Tomorrow, you'll cash your first check. Baby on the way, remember? Won't come cheap, that little critter. She stands, walks over to me and runs a finger along my cheek.

Let's get this over with, my brother says, tugging my arm.

Outside, the narcocorridos play on, and my brother's car is already purring in the driveway.

I would squirt a few drops into that eye of yours, my brother says, opening the passenger door for me. You don't want to be meeting the secretary of defense looking like a drug addict.

I get in the car and wait for him to go around before responding, This thing in my eye is immune to whatever is poured into it.

This line of work is also a game of appearances.

I wouldn't mind getting out of this car if that'd work best.

Oh, no, but the firstborn must learn, right?

What's in the back, Alex?

No big deal. A few high-caliber collectibles, bottle of high-end Cognac, a briefcase filled with cash. Gifts so the secretary can have his fun and not stand in the way of our operation.

So, this is something you do often?

And there you were asking *me* to realize the country I live in.

Now I see why you have those big, crooked fangs.

You won't last, big brother. You can call it quits right now, and I'll drop you off at the bookstore.

Don't tempt me.

Oh, but *baby on the way*, right? *Won't come cheap that little critter*. Is that why you're sticking it out?

That obvious?

If you only knew how hard Mom has worked for this business.

Before crafting a response, which would probably involve

the clairvoyant and tarot cards, my phone pings and shoots its blinding light. I close my bad eye and read my wife's message:
How's my symbolist arms dealer doing?
He's found that he has extinguished all human hope from his soul.
Ha Ha! Funny.
Nothing Ha Ha about it, misfortune is my god.
She stops responding after that, and I turn the phone over to avoid the light from the screen.

47

We drive towards the city, where the haze hangs above it with an opaque glow. In my mind's eye, where images remain clear and fully defined, I see my wife cutting her paper trees, while the sky can't help but feed on our everyday residues.

Past the toll booth, where this time my brother pays with company funds, dusk begins to change its color. The exact hour when light and darkness meet, making the headlights invisible in front of us. The light that does eventually flood into our car comes in winks, red and blue, paired with the urgent wail of a police siren, louder as it tails us. A voice asks us to pull over through the loudspeaker's cough.

While an electric tingle runs down my body, my brother just says, Fuck.

What do you mean *fuck*? After what you said earlier, I would think you'd have a situation like this covered.

Shut up and open the glove compartment. Hand me the envelope.

I'm surprised by how fast I move, slipping the envelope straight into his suit pocket.

Just stay calm and keep your face that way. With two fingers, he points to his eyes and then straight ahead.

The siren has gone quiet behind us, but the lights keep up their bicolored loop. In the rearview, I see the policeman stride towards us. He then leans on the car window and asks for my brother's license and registration, which he already has prepared in his right hand.

The policeman asks him to step out of the car, which he does, and I can already foresee the popping of the trunk, the gold-plated collectibles in the hands of the policeman, the oceanic amber of the Cognac in the bottle, pictures of my brother's face and mine on the news, next to the confiscated cash. The federal forces boasting our arrest, my wife watching me on the TV, lonesome and pregnant from our bed.

But the conversation between my brother and the policeman continues cordially, full of puns and laughter.

Night falls black over the land, and they keep at their negotiation. The red and blue lights spill even more vibrantly into the car. The rearview only allows me a cropped image, but it does offer the suggestion of my brother pulling that envelope from his suit. I cover my bad eye—more laughter and then an overstated embrace with three taps on the policeman's back, exactly like the one the American-Faux-Stridentist gave me the evening of his reading.

My brother returns to the car, buckles up. Then three taps on the bodywork signal we are allowed to carry on.

He winks at me from the driver's seat, and the police car overtakes us, its lights sinking in the sloping bends ahead.

What was in that envelope?

What do you think?

I shake my head and look out my window towards the sliding night and the even darker silhouette of bushy trees.

We should fucking sell this business.

Yeah, yeah, holy holy, my brother says, a smug smile showcasing his canine fangs. Now perk up. Ready to meet one of the real hotshots?

Yeah, Alex, cannot fucking wait.

48

Friday morning has me in the foggy depths of a hangover, a banging, gong-like headache reverberating in the back of my skull.

Last night, the secretary of defense demanded we partake in a couple glasses of the ill-fated Cognac. One snifter of the liquor, filled with notes of cashews and dates, rapidly turned to a second and a third while the secretary of defense joked with my brother about my appearance, *your new, harmless bodyguard,* adding that my pterygium did give him somewhat of a scare at first sight. The bottle slowly drained away, the liquor running past the plumper part of the pear-shaped bottle with the insignia of our family guns.

When he led us to the door, past which my brother's car was bathed by weak moonlight, he hugged my brother goodbye, fumbling his new gold-plated gun, cartridge full and loaded. I tried to move away from the darting tip of that cannon until he pulled me in and gave me a slight pat on the shoulder. Turning to my brother, holding the gun limply from the trigger's hook, he said, Get your fucking bodyguard some nicer clothes.

Surreal as it was, it feels like a distant memory as my wife wakes me well past eight in the morning, the traffic on the streets already blaring loudly beneath our window.

No work today, Arthur? Smells like a shattered bottle of whiskey in here.

I rub my bad eye and then press the lower end of my palm against my forehead. It was Cognac, I tell her, and fake a regurgitating sound.

Made some coffee, she says, pulling the covers away from me. Bought the Ethiopian kind you love. She tosses the fleecy robe she used before she was pregnant over me, which I slide into effortlessly.

The Ethiopian coffee is, indeed, succulent. Every sip covers the lingering taste of Cognac in my mouth. Standing over her mock-up, I notice there are now trees over other trees, the lane reserved for them already full, but this city of ours needs more of them or, better yet, needs to be left for ruin, for the thicket to grow over it, for the underbrush to conquer from within, left there for future generations as the shining example of civilizational suicide. A sudden commotion outside takes my sight from the mock-up to the section of street framed by our window. The Famous-Armless-Writer is sprinting down the sidewalk, wearing, as always, his long, hooded overcoat. He disappears behind the street that leads to the Mercado Juárez, his dogs nowhere in sight.

My wife joins me at the window and pours more coffee into my mug.

Did you see that? I ask her.

See what?

Our neighbor, the writer—*La Santa Muerte*.

She scans the street, shakes her head, and pours more coffee into her mug too.

Coffee is OK? I ask, placing my hand on her belly. With the diet, I mean.

She nods. Two cups a day. She has another sip, then wipes her lips with the back of her hand. Should I run the shower for you? I'm getting drunk just from the smell you're oozing.

I have a long swig of coffee, then say, No time. El Harar awaits. Payment day is here.

Eye drops, at least? This hangover of yours isn't helping that lovely eye.

I'm starting to think that what we need is some acceptance. Look at your trees there. Perhaps some things will just *be*.

She winces, shakes her head, and sits down next to her mock-up, cutting up more of her green papier-mâché.

Once I'm out on the street, the pain now sharp in the middle of my forehead, it seems like the Famous-Armless-Writer is racing a few blocks ahead—a vanishing, hurrying ghost. On every lamppost on the way to the Metrobús, a poster with the faces of the men sequestered by the army offers rewards for any sort of information about them. Eleven faces plastered all over the city, each with their full name underneath, faces and names that linger all throughout my public transport journey to El Harar. In the living room, my brother is sipping on a michelada, and my mother is sitting on her lounger.

There you are, she says. That Cognac was a gift, not for you two to gobble down.

I shake my head. I wish I could've refused it. But you should've seen Alex playing the sommelier, swirling the liquor in the glass, sticking that big nose of his in it.

Very funny, my brother says, and sips, his lips gathering bits of salt from the thick ring along the rim of the glass. On the desk behind him are two envelopes with our names on them, which I can't take my sight from.

Go on, my mother says, just take it already, and take the rest of the day off—you look and smell like a clochard.

I reach for the envelope and slip out the check. An unexpected amount of zeroes swivel and turn on the paper until I shut my right eye. Dang, I say, this is just a week's worth? Then turning to my brother, I add, Is this what you've been making all along, you smug motherfucker? Suddenly being held at gunpoint seems worth it.

I obviously make more than you do, idiot, my brother says, sparking my mother's laughter beside him.

Heading out the door, my phone pings.

Juicy payment for your services, Arthur?

Let's just say that the only unbearable thing is that nothing is unbearable.

49

After cooking a wholesome brunch of vegan pancakes with maple-flavored agave syrup and tofu bacon for my wife and our lazy daughter inside her, I head for my scheduled weekend meeting with the Would-Be-Writer, whose text message this morning forecasts bad news, *I'll tell you all about it in person. I'm not a happy camper.*

On my way over, my first strides through the neighborhood make me question not only my sight but my sanity: below the posters with the faces of the sequestered men, the faces of the Famous-Armless-Writer's dogs are also posted on every lamppost, their names clear in bold text, GIDE AND LORD ALFRED.

The word REWARD now doubled on every block, I find it hard not to be baffled by how the amount offered is ridiculous relative to what I made for a week's worth at El Harar. I'm also left to wonder if this happened on the day that I tossed the pebble at those dogs when they tried to follow my path. I turn every which way to see if the Famous-Armless-Writer's vanishing figure is in sight, but Marsella Street is mostly empty.

The Would-Be-Writer picked a café in my neighborhood with long communal tables and the sound of classical music as background, whose offering of coffee comes in a variety of preparations, from a Japanese siphon to a six-minute pour over, every roasted bean sourced in the high altitudes of the Mexican coffee belt at fair-trade prices. On the sidewalk right in front of the café, a woman sells tacos, tamales, and Nescafé in a stand specked with rust, all of them at a fraction of what we have to pay here. The few nuisances: the hiss of her fryer, the strings of smoke heading skyward in their fading twirl.

My doppio sets me back fifty pesos and sixty more for the Would-Be-Writer's pour over sourced in the mountains of Cuetzalan. He lets me slide his coffee in front of him, apparently assuming it's my treat.

Having the first scalding sip, he gurgles the black liquid and nods in appreciation. Good, yeah?

I like my Ethiopian at home better, especially on weekends, and especially with my pregnant wife.

To each his own, *to each his own*.

I take my seat. So, what is it that's making you *not a happy camper*? I say, adding air quotes.

Well, what would you like first, the bad news or the *worst* news?

This steals a laugh from me, although his neutral reaction gives away that humor was the least of his intentions. You pick, I tell him.

Both book-related, by the way.

I was assuming *and* hoping so.

So, remember my collaborator's dogs?

I hiss out through my nose, a sound not dissimilar to the frying outside.

They ran out. They're lost.

I can't restrain the rush of a small chuckle.

And somehow this is funny to you.

No, I just kind of figured that one out by walking around the neighborhood.

He shakes his head, in confusion it seems, so I step out of the café and rip one of the MISSING DOG posters from a lamppost to show it to him.

He studies the picture for a second, his eyes serious, his forehead furrowed, then puts the poster aside and takes another sip from his coffee. Turning back up to me, he says, Well, the man is losing his mind. Wants to put anything to do with the book on hold.

Well, understandably. He's too busy dashing around the neighborhood at soaring speeds.

You *do* see the problem we have here?

We?

I've already agreed to a launch date, my aunt is the director at the Museum of Modern Art, and I already booked the space for the night of the reading.

But his text is done already, edited, reedited, squeaky clean, if you ask me.

It's hard to tell if he feels offended by this. After all, the editing of this book has been a true balancing act, trying to frame these guys as peers.

But I need him there, he says. The publisher wants him there—there's no book without him. He is one of the parts.

I nod along, thinking he is more like the *crucial* part, the justifier.

So, he says, I was thinking, maybe, we should set up a brigade, a search team or whatever, and look around for those dogs. He raises the poster with their faces.

This time, a very earnest laugh escapes me. Sorry, but what makes you think they haven't already been reduced to taco meat at that food stand? I point to the lady outside, who rips open a plastic bag of raw meat and drops it into the popping oil bubbles of her hotplate. Beside her, a wolf-like mutt sniffs the fallen remnants of food, doubtfully, then turns away, Perro no come perro, you know.

Look, man, be as snarky as you want. You are part of this book too. You've been paid, up-front.

Exactly. Let's talk about the book, then. I'm certainly not here to talk about dog brigades. I'll let you pursue that project on your own.

Oh, so you want to talk about the *worst* news. Is that it?

A heaviness comes over me, and I can't fight the cavernous

yawn forming. Once my face reverts to its usual shape, I say, Yes, let's hear *the worst news.*

He pulls out the manuscript, which I see is now full of his own notes, marked with the odd shade of sky-blue ink. I'm finding it hard to see myself in here, he says.

I wince at him, hoping he has the shrewdness to see I'm looking doubtful.

You've been too prescriptive. You're almost erasing me and my brother from the book.

You *do* know that the document gives you the option to reject my edits, line by line?

But it's like you've rewritten the whole damn thing. Where am *I*?

Then write everything over! These suggestions are what you pay me for. I pause, finish my doppio in one gulp, which by now tastes like warm lemon juice. Look, this is standard editing. Your words needed to be polished. The story is always there. Every story has already been told—sure, you can be autobiographical. That's fine, but real writing means molding all that into shape, casting it in a certain light.

He sips his coffee, speechless.

Look, I say. True alchemy lies in this formula: Your memory and your senses are only the nourishment, the fuel for your creative impulse. But there's a lot of work to be done after that.

He nods, wincing.

Now, if you can't even manage that, good luck with your dog brigade.

50

My wife and I wake up moments before dawn to the blast of the Mexican martial tune I last heard in elementary school. In my disoriented state, unable to properly place the latest events on a linear timeline—the mouth of that rifle trained on me, the pterygium on the admiral's eye, the young men seized by the army, the gold-plated gun in the fumbling hands of the drunken secretary of defense, the missing dogs—I walk to the window, trembling with fear, as if I have suddenly become a target of the armed forces, from whom there is really no place to hide.

Our electronic clock beams 6:00 a.m. on the dot, red and bright. When I flick open the shades, the martial tune becomes louder. From bed, my wife screams, What's happening? her voice wavering in fearsome highs and lows like the trumpets outside.

It's OK, I tell her through the whine of music as I watch the uniformed men and women of our armed forces march down Marsella Street. The procession soon gains in numbers: first the small lineup of six men guarding the flag, which hangs limply from its silver poll, then the group grows, like the immediate shift from drizzle to downpour—a flood of soldiers fills the street outside our window. The final contingents take up the width of the street, the drumrolls and the blare of the trumpets ebbing in the distance. Behind the last line of soldiers, what looks like the Famous-Armless-Writer's dogs try to cross the street through the mass, but they flinch at the stomping of military boots, and terrified, they run away in the opposite direction. I turn back towards our bed. You OK?

No, my wife says. Something doesn't feel right. The pressure gauge that the pediatrician gave us hangs idle in her hands. As I walk towards her, the sound outside dies away, and the pale light of dawn slowly breaks through the shades.

51

Come Monday morning, the phones are going off nonstop at El Harar: some rumble, some ring; our cellphones chirp with their cicada whirs. On the other end, it's mostly journalists demanding interviews. Somehow, news that we visited the secretary of defense's home seeped through the cracks. There is footage that proves it, and the questions are endless: what was the meeting about? Did we agree to a new contract to supply the armed forces?

Is the secretary of defense a private client? Was the meeting related to the latest news stating that the confiscated weapons and bullet shells at the crime scene matched our brand? Do we believe in transparency? Do we find it ethical to sell to undisclosed clients given the drug war that engulfs the country?

During a rare bit of silence, I turn to my brother. What should I say?

Just be polite and proper. Buy us some time. Say they're guns from Walmart up north, *Fast and Furious*, or what have you.

You mean be a cynical and hypocritical lying sack of shit?

Call it what you want, he says, typing with freakish speed on his phone. Just don't shoot yourself in the foot.

The journalist that called me before, right after the news of the carnage broke, remains resilient. Declining the call doesn't put him off. The phone continues vibrating on the wooden surface of my desk. I tap the green button on the screen and speak quickly before even hearing what he has to say, How many times do I have to say this? Wrong number.

I hang up, but the screen comes alive instantly with another private call, so I decline and turn my cellphone off.

Swift learner, my brother says, giving me a fish-hooked smile. Who would've known?

Where is Mother, anyway? I ask, collapsing on the couch. Maybe *she* should deal with all this.

Said she'd be busy for a few days. That we shouldn't pester, and show our worth.

Just makes us seem guilty, you know.

We *are* guilty, remember, of bribery, at least.

I run both hands through my hair. So, what if we come clean? Is it illegal to come bearing gifts for our friends? Is it illegal to sell to undisclosed clients?

I won't even pretend to answer those questions.

Oh, for fuck's sake, Alex. So what happens now?

We wait for things to quiet down.

What if they don't?

With that, his phone rings, and he lifts a finger, asking me to hold my thoughts. He answers with a wry smile, looking straight at me. How are you? He says into the receiver. How's the pregnancy coming along? You know I'm dying to be an uncle.

A shiver spreads down my torso while my brother taps the speakerphone button, and my wife's voice streams from it. So, how's my Arthur Rimbaud doing? Is he there? Can't reach him on his phone.

Arthur Rimbaud? my brother says. More like Arthur Rambo!

My wife laughs on the other end. Right, she says.

He's right here, listening.

Can you hand him the phone? she says, in a voice now out of patience.

My brother tosses it to me, and I disable speakerphone. Everything all right?

I don't know, she says. I've moved up our visit to the pediatrician's. I need you to meet me there soon.

I turn to look at my brother while I listen and nod. Just tell me everything's OK.

I can't. I need to hear that myself. I think my blood pressure's up. Don't be late.

I hang up, toss the cellphone back to my brother, and pull my jacket over my shoulders. I'll leave you to your cynicism and hypocrisy, seems like you're in your element.

No, no, he says, wagging a finger. What makes you think you can leave?

My daughter. You can't stop me.

He shakes his head in resignation and keeps on texting.

Once outside, the drizzle begins its daily descent, the silvery needles falling at a slant. I follow the gravel path to the gate, and once outside the walls of El Harar, a few journalists snap their cameras at me and encircle me with microphones. I begin a slight dash to break off from them, the cameras flashing behind me. In the distance, the bus rumbles towards the stop, so I sprint ahead and wave it down. As the bus waits for me, its muffler puffs out black smoke, which disappears as it gains height. The bus rolls forward as soon as I set foot on it, the rain now louder on its roof. I can feel my heart under my skin, its quick, heavy beats. I sit in the only available seat on the back end of the bus, where a woman is shuffling tarot cards in her hands. Turning to face her, a knot grows and fastens in my throat, and I'm on the verge of asking her about my mother, our death sentence, Holy Death looking over the Fallen Tower, but my stare only makes her put the cards away, then rise and stumble her way to the front of the bus. At the following stop, she gets off. With the bus in motion, she slips away and shrinks behind the back window. Through the film of water rushing down the glass, I watch the blur of her figure walk down a slender path lined by thicket, the hazy sepia backdrop of Mexico City at the far end.

52

I arrive late to the pediatrician's office thanks to the lunchtime rush hour. The secretary gives me her *where have you been?* look, pursed lips and rolling eyes, which deserves no response. I blow past her into the pink and blue room, where my wife is laying on her back on the bed, gleaming lines of tears streaming down her cheeks. The pediatrician is holding her hand like I should be doing, offering the reassuring words, There's no reason to panic. This happens, we've dealt with it successfully in the past.

My body is hot, my mouth dry, and my face has surely lost all its color at this sight, at hearing the words, Where the hell were you? springing forth from my wife's throat—a wavering, desperate cry.

I dash towards her, and the pediatrician dodges me. I kneel to grab hold of her sweaty palms. What's wrong? What's going on?

Her chest balloons. She heaves a sigh. Where the hell were you? she says again, softer this time, more of a despaired hiss.

Traffic, protests, paparazzi at the door, I left as soon as we spoke. I kiss her hand held tight in my grip, run the back of it over my cheek. With my other hand, I run the palm over her belly.

What's happening?

Blood pressure is sky high, tipping towards hypertension, the pediatrician says behind me. We've given her some medicine to bring it back down.

It's OK, I tell her, all good.

Beside her bed, one of the pediatrician's iPads comes to life with a jovial song spewing from the mouth of an animated pony, which he taps to silence.

Your daughter still hasn't turned, he says, speaking loudly over my wife's heavy breathing. We have to keep an eye out for pre-eclampsia moving forward. Then turning to my wife and placing a hand on her head, he says, We're treating this as a high-risk pregnancy from now on, and if your pressure keeps on spiking, we might have to induce labor.

What do you mean *induce*? I say. We're still over a month away.

My wife's tears are now rolling down my hands. The pediatrician's hand is still resting on her head, petting her like the Famous-Armless-Writer used to pet his dogs.

We'll take zero risks. If she has to come out, she comes out. If she still hasn't turned, we do a C-section. We need to look after this beautiful woman too.

I feel myself nodding, my wife's hand still hot on my cheek.

Now, the pediatrician says, we'll need a urine sample before you leave.

My wife keeps nodding, mechanically and quickly, wiping tears from her face.

Once you get home, you're to stay in bed until we deliver your baby, whenever that may be. And we'll have a nurse on call at your nearest clinic, monitoring your situation four times a day, starting tonight. He unwraps a cup from a plastic bag and shakes it in his hand. Time to pee, he says, handing it to my wife, who keeps at her swift nodding, and letting go of my hand, she rises from the bed.

Looking up at her, I ask, You want me to go with you?

You want to come watch me pee?

I nod slightly.

No, please don't, she says, and disappears behind the bathroom door.

We hear a muffled hum after she turns on the light inside. A few seconds later, we can clearly hear the stream of her urine, first against the water pooled at the bottom of the toilet, then louder against the plastic cup.

53

We have moved the drafting table next to our bed, her mock-up too, which is now even more cluttered with art deco buildings and miniature trees. We have bought an endless supply of green papier-mâché, along with new scissors, cutters, glue, anything she might need to press on with the construction of her utopias, the possible, albeit unfathomable, world that awaits our reticent daughter. We've also bought another paper roll, fifty yards in length, long enough to fit her mad-scientist formulas with the black ink of her Sharpie.

Lying in bed with her—dividing my blurry sight between her scribbles and the Would-Be-Writer's text on my laptop's screen with the growing leak, which bears a now uncanny resemblance to the shape of our sitting baby—her moods swing like a pendulum.

Sometimes I feel like she's angry, she says, turning to me, Like she's going on strike, like she knows about this world out here with its ozone-gray skies.

Come on, she's just lazy and snug in there. I lean my head over her womb, listening to the palpitation of our daughter inside her, sounds like the welling of a storm.

Well, that's what I mean. She wipes the first tear that rolls from the dam of her eyelid. She has a premonition of what *out here* is, this living hell.

Living hell? I lift my face from her warm belly to meet her eyes. I don't know about *living hell*.

Murdered people buried in pits, exhaust fumes for air, a half-blind arms-dealing poet for a father—and she surrenders to a wild laugh I didn't see coming.

Whoa there! That does sound like the worst part of it.

She expels another laugh, of the spitting kind this time.

I'd refuse coming out too, I say.

But then she falls quiet, ominously, adjusting her expression to a temporary, eerie calm. She shakes her head. I don't know . . .

Look, it's not like she has a choice. I run the back of my fingers along her wet cheek. She'll come out, whether she likes it or not.

She nods but erratically, pursing her lips, her eyes darting in every direction. I'm afraid of her resistance.

I kiss her belly. She'll be a tough activist like her mother then.

She breathes out through another nod, and I sit back up when my laptop emits a ping, signaling a new message. I place it on my lap and struggle to see past the leak. In a new email, the Would-Be-Writer informs me that he finally spoke to the Famous-Armless-Writer, who now wants to add a chapter to the book about his lost dogs.

Fuck's sake, I whisper and turn to my wife again.

She reaches over and runs a finger over the black leak, rubbing the spot where the screen is shattered, where our daughter's heart would be if she were the leak.

I broke it, she says. Now you can't write your book.

Her words have me looking for the folder where I saved my symbolist poems, the ones she liked, but it must be somewhere behind that leak, drowned in the flood, lost, never to wash up again.

The black night, it consumed it, she says.

I swallow and nod.

She tears a yard of paper from her roll and slides it over my lap, then uncaps her Sharpie and holds it before me. Here, she says, write of silences, of nights . . .

Then my voice joins hers to cap off the sentence, *Tie down the vertigo.*

Yes. She nods. Write your own. Stop editing that bullshit book for someone else.

54

Come morning, I only rise from bed due to the impending burst of my bladder. A weakness has taken hold of me. Chills run down every inch of my skin, which is beyond feverish.

After releasing a reeking and syrupy yellow stream of piss, I look at my ghostly reflection in the mirror. My pterygium has grown—at the pace, it seems, of the leak in my computer—giving the vision in my right eye the quality of an unfocused lens. After splashing water on my face and rubbing my eyes, I return to bed, frowning and moaning, Feel like seven shades of shit here.

What's wrong, Arthur? my wife asks, her voice tired, eyes veiled behind her sleep mask.

Got chills, must have a fever or something.

She breathes out long, lifts the mask so it rests on her forehead but keeps her eyes shut.

But how are *you* feeling? I ask.

She places a thumb over the veins in her wrist, So far, so good, I think. You'll have to take my pressure, she says, already reaching blindly for the gauge and fastening it around her bicep. It takes only three pumps to turn the needle full swing. Still hyper-tense, but not at alarming levels. Enough, though, to make my temperature rise one more degree while feeling another sweeping shiver run throughout my body.

Yet another day in the confines of this bed, she says.

Seems like I could use one.

Skipping work, are you?

Can't go all the way over there like this. I'm calling in sick.

I walk over to fetch my phone, which seems to hide from me behind the blur in my eye. Wincing, then covering my bad eye for focus, I text my brother.

You can't be serious, he texts back instantly, and on the screen, I can see that he is already typing a new message.

Useless wimp! Shit's raining down on us.

I chuck the phone back onto the desk and head back to bed, veering around the drafting table. I then wrap myself tightly in the covers, belching out painfully.

I hope it's not the typhus, Arthur.

Very funny. I barely turn to face her. Feel like shit here, truth be told.

Yes, you said that already. She shrugs. Welcome to my world.

Turning my back to her and pulling the covers over half my face, I fall into a brief dream that is like a spliced reel of otherworldly images: the clairvoyant on the bus sinking her hands in our Ethiopian coffee, my mother walking the Famous-Armless-Writer's dogs, me consoling my brother as he sits on Mother's favorite chair. Scenes that are interrupted by the rumbling vibration of my phone, the words *Gun lords calling* from a voice I soon recognize as my wife's.

When I'm fully awake, I find her working on a formula on the paper roll, spidery numbers next to indecipherable Greek letters.

Aren't you going to take that call? she says.

Just pushing myself upright brings a tender pain to my every muscle. It's probably just that journalist.

The phone goes still but then comes alive again. I reach over for it to find the word *Mother* on the screen. I swipe to answer.

What's with you? Are you drunk again?

Sick . . . the fever.

She scoffs, The unreliable children I reared. There's a slice of silence that is quickly shattered by the rumbling of a truck outside our window. When it fades, she says, You better get your ass here tomorrow morning. I don't care what shape you're in. I have important news.

As she hangs up, another image of that clairvoyant comes to me—the real one, not the image slanted by my unconscious—the image of how she stumbled down the aisle of that bus to get away from me, cards safely tucked in her purse.

Can't catch a fucking break, I say, to who, I don't know, but my wife eyes me knowingly. I know, I tell her, I know, and the following noise is that of our bolt unlocking—my wife's nurse and her timely arrival.

I'm asked downstairs so they can perform the daily checkup.

Not even coffee tempts me in this state, so all I do is stare out the window, where the sun fails to break over the cloud of gray smog. The blur in my eye catches the rare pools of light and amplifies them, iridescent spots at once kaleidoscopic and blinding.

After some minutes, I make out the figure of the Famous-Armless-Writer power walking down our block, turning every which way, looking for his dogs. Following his path, lagging behind, the Would-Be-Writer cranes his neck in every direction, sticking two fingers into his mouth and blowing out a high-pitched whistle. From his coat pocket, he pulls out more MISSING DOGS signs, tapes them to every other wall. Gide! Lord Alfred! he yells, and then disappears as he turns the corner.

55

When I get to El Harar the next morning, my mother is again sitting in her favorite chair; her face is paler than usual. All around her, an eerie and celestial white light shoots down from the skylight, its beams also shining marginally over my brother, who is sitting on the desk beside her, going over a stack of papers, wetting the tip of his finger before turning the pages. Barely looking at me, he says, Will there ever come a day when you arrive on time?

I turn to him briefly but return my sight to my mother, You said you had news.

She breathes in long, stares at her watch. That can wait. Then turning to my brother, she adds, Something far more important has come up.

Please tell me we're selling, I say, rubbing my eye, thinking of slipping my sunglasses back on—the glare indoors rendering the scene particulate, fuzzy.

You wish, my brother says, lifting the stack of pages and tapping them on the sides like I do with the Would-Be-Writer's manuscript. He extends the bulk in my direction, which I refuse to take.

Do I even want to lay eyes on that?

How does it look, Alex? My mother cuts in.

Looks like we'll have nothing to worry about financially in the coming year, my brother says, forcing the pages into my hands and then sitting back down, crossing a leg, letting an idiotic smile spread across his face.

Shutting my bad eye and looking over the cover page of the document, I soon realize it's an ammunition order scheduled over a one-year period, with a bolded seven-figure number at the bottom of the page. With every passing month, the vertical column shows an exponential growth in the number of bullets we are to ship to different spots in the country, as far north as Tijuana, as far east as Veracruz, and to the edge of the Pacific Coast in Lázaro Cardenas, Michoacán. The one thing not immediately clear is who the client is—the white space on the page reserved for the name has been left blank.

Who sent this?

Just came in, my brother says, via the Department of Defense. I'm sure they can vouch for whoever needs the ammo.

Whoever? These are bullets we're selling.

Look, my mother says, outstretching an arm in my direction, you're our ammunition representative, yes? She then turns briefly to my brother, whose eye roll is so dramatic his eyes go as white as the empty space on the order for a second. Read it over. Make a decision. That's what I pay you for, isn't it?

Like I can actually decline the offer, I say. Alex, here, has already drooled over every sheet of paper.

Like I said, it's *your* jurisdiction, *your* decision to make, my mother says. I want a full report and a decision by the end of the week.

Sure as hell, the daily patter of rain begins once again. On the skylight, solitary pecks at first, then urgent tinks cover every inch of land outside. Under the sound of the rain comes three knocks on the door—a longer pause between the first two, like a code—and my mother rises hurriedly from her seat to answer.

She walks over to the door, pulls it open—the lashing of the rain suddenly much louder—and there is a long embrace.

Led by my mother's hand, the clairvoyant steps into the living room, already expertly shuffling a deck of cards in her left hand. A few drops of rain have pearled on her long, orange tunic. Stopping before me, she stares into my eyes without blinking, in what can only be described as a look of defiance, making me suddenly very aware of my heavy heartbeat.

Now, off you go, my mother says, waving me and my brother towards the door, both of you. There's work to be done, and she taps the pages in my hand.

I take a step towards the door but then stop. Maybe *she* should read this, I say, turning and pointing the pages at the clairvoyant. Ask the cards.

The clairvoyant keeps on staring and then smiles, causing me to avert my eyes. Taking a few steps in my direction, my mother says, Show some respect. Her words are more air than voice. Now get out of here. She takes me by the shoulders and spins me in the direction of the door.

Walking away, I recall those coffee beans, those grains of rice, and my mind conjures up the clear image of a fallen tower. I relive the dream of bullets in my coffee grinder and then turn once more before crossing the threshold to stare at this woman who hopped off the bus when I sat next to her, whose image slipped behind the wet windows as the bus gained speed.

But as I step into the rain, I think of my wife's pregnant belly, the paper trees lined up on top of it. Then it's my daughter, mercurial on the black ultrasound screen, sitting in her refusal, already full of loathing for this world.

56

Next morning, riding in the back of the taxi on my way to El Harar, the radio spews out the findings of a recent journalistic investigation into the causes of this unprecedented decline in the quality of the air. This ever-present pollution, which is composed of a concentration of carbon monoxide, ozone, and every other floating toxic particle, has us living under a cloud of smog similar to those in India, China, and the Philippines. Countries, much like our city these days, where the sun is a mere suggestion behind the haze, where they live in a state of constant dusk.

The report has found that the recent levels of smog are directly connected to a string of events caused by criminals and the corrupted clockwork of the country: the cartels control large swaths of the territory and have become experts of economic diversification. They are now making huge profits by selling huachicol —gasoline stolen from state-long Pemex pipelines—across the northern border. The immediate solution to the lack of national gasoline has been the importation of cheap and adulterated gasoline from China, a piece of information which the government has been sure to keep on the down-low, and now that it has surfaced and has been exposed by mass media, they are not releasing any comments about it. What they *have* done, via the scapegoat holding the title of secretary of energy, is to announce that to clear the alarming levels of ozone in the air, one-fifth of the cars in the city will be banned for one day a week in a rotation according to the first numbers on their license plates. This news has my taxi driver shaking his head full swing.

The fucking crooks, he says, catching my sight in the rearview.

I give him a slow nod, The fucking crooks, indeed—an agreement that earns me the silence I crave for the remainder of the drive.

When he drops me off at El Harar, there's already a misty cloud encircling the hills, and in the driveway, my brother's car is slick with dew.

Inside the office, there's a fresh litter of coffee and rice on the rug, accumulating in larger mounds around my mother's chair.

Fuck's sake, I tell my brother, who is lying flat on the couch, both sets of fingers pressing against his temples. What? We'll all die now, is that it? Every bearer of the name?

Have you gone over the ammunition order? he asks.

That's what I'm here to do.

We have to approve it. Something just doesn't feel right.

Yeah, I say, moving his feet aside so I can sit on the couch. Perhaps what's wrong is that the order is anonymous.

He sighs, then reaches down to collect some coffee beans and toss them at me. *This*, you idiot. Seems like we're in the hands of that clairvoyant, like she'll crush us at her will.

Come on, Alex, I'm sure Mother knows better.

Oh, right. With his shoe, he pushes around rice and coffee. Fickle is what she is.

Where is she anyway? I'd think she'd be all over my case with this.

That's what I mean! he shouts and abruptly stands. I need a walk. He goes into his office to fetch his handgun before storming out towards the shooting range.

Fully reclining onto the couch, I take advantage of the silence to go over the details of the order.

The request is structured over a one-year period made up of monthly payments and weekly deliveries. The number of bullets— three different calibers, both in their regular and expanding varieties—rises each month to levels that could not only nurture the United States' oil wars in the Middle East but also the exponential cartel bloodshed we watch on the news every evening. As I had suspected, the elephant in the room continues to be the order's anonymity, which makes my stomach stir with unease. I try my mother's cell over and over again to no avail.

Outside, our daily downpour begins, chasing my brother from the shooting range all the way back inside before he is able to fire a single blast from his gun. Once inside, he removes his coat and pats his damp hair.

Is this really my jurisdiction? I ask him.

He exhales impatiently and walks to his desk to stick his handgun in the drawer.

Alex, is this really my decision to make?

I don't think it should be.

An anonymous order in a country with a death toll that's rising past a hundred thousand. This is bad. Do you even watch the news?

He searches for a response but just shrugs.

This means no background check, I say. We could be arming anybody.

Like your beloved Rimbaud in Ethiopia.

Can we be serious here for a second?

You already know how I feel about it. You know my opinion. He shuffles around the room, opening every drawer in his desk and finally grabbing his car keys.

Then you'll have to live with mine.

You want to make this tower crumble, go right ahead. He yanks his coat back on erratically, struggling to get his arms into the sleeves. You're playing into that clairvoyant's hands with this nonsense of yours, he says, finally forcing his arms through with the sound of ripping fabric. He heads for the door, pulls it open with a thump, then appears behind the frame of the window, battered by rain until he gets into his car.

When the Audi A6 is lost behind the gates, I return to the order, but I'm immediately interrupted by the loud ring of the land line. I pick up, hoping it's my mother, but my mouth goes dry when I hear the hoarse voice on the other side of the line: Cartel Jalisco Nueva Generación, hang up and you're a dead man walking.

Surely, he can hear my breath, loud and fearful, on the other end of the line.

Listen, the man says. You are to decline the order you have in your hands.

The blurry vision of my right eye has me trying to pinpoint details outside the window. Am I being watched? Are they right outside these adobe walls?

Think of your family, their safety.

My whole body is laced with sweat. I hang up the phone with a slam and rise from my desk. Heading for the door, I try my mother's and my brother's numbers again, but both immediately go to voicemail.

Outside, the air is cool and wet, and my only thought is to get out, to sprint into the rain, into its loud rattle. The horizon trembles with every step over the cumbersome gravel.

In a valiant leap, I'm past El Harar's gate, onto the empty road, waiting to be plucked from the land, then buried in one of those mass graves scattered all over the country.

Sitting on the concrete steps at the bus stop, my viscera hollow, I shut my eyes until I hear the rumbling of the bus's engine coming through the rain, until its wheels run through the puddles at my feet.

Think of your family, the voice said, and now all I can think of is my wife, sitting alone in our bed, and my daughter inside her mouthing the words, *I told you so*.

57

I switch to a cab once the bus enters the city, but the traffic jam near our duplex forces me to abandon the nicotine-reeking Nissan Sentra, and I begin sprinting down the median strip of Avenida Chapultepec, which, as Homero Aridjis notes in *La Leyenda de los Soles,* no longer seems to have been built on the ground but rather over a thick accumulation of low-lying smog.

Turning left on Marsella Street, I slow down at the sight of a pack of stray dogs barking at me. They have taken over the width of the sidewalk. The Famous-Armless-Writer's dogs are sitting right in the middle of the pack. I pick up a pebble just in case and cross the street, heading straight for our duplex, the voice behind that phone call loud in my mind.

Opening the door to complete silence, I find the blinds pulled all the way down but allowing thin shafts of light in. The stairs lead me up to an even darker bedroom. The mock-up is a cluttered silhouette on the drafting table next to our bed, where my wife is covered in a heap of blankets, her face pressed into the pillow, a thin needle of exterior light creeping across her stomach like a slash.

I switch on the lights to see her more clearly, wincing at the yellow outpour from every bulb, an electric feeling running through my limbs.

With the room fully bathed in light, I notice that my wife's paper roll is full and that she has started writing on the walls— mad scientist formulas growing exponentially, a mass of numbers, letters, and signs. Silently, I bring my ear close to her nose to catch her breathing. Honey, I say, and she breathes out harder, the rushing air tickling my ear. I move down to her stomach and listen to my daughter, the furious pulse of her life.

58

After my mother heard about the extortion call, she managed to negotiate an armored car and a few members of the National Guard to drive my brother and me to El Harar. Behind the thick, tinted windows, the streets are already half empty; there is no traffic on the roads, but the pollution is far from receding. The city sliding by resembles the world painted by Aridjis: deadly and dark, a true magical realist dystopia where it seems like half the population of our beloved city has perished and the few people out on the street are nothing but ghosts. The news from the radio heightens this sense of doom—the secretary of education has ordered a mandatory suspension of classes because the ozone in the air has reached levels that pose serious health risks to children.

When we get to El Harar, coffee and rice still litter the living room. Again, the gun matriarch is nowhere to be found, but she has left our checks on her desk. Ripping the envelope open, I see that she has deducted payment for the days I missed.

The ammunition order throbs on my desk, and my brother shifts his eyes towards it, then turns to me before looking down at his phone.

Not done with it yet, Alex. I haven't decided.

Yeah, yeah, take your time. It *is* the end of the week, though. Better press on.

The ring of the telephone quiets him. He picks up, brings the phone to his ear, and then hangs up in a quick, definite movement. He exhales, troubled.

Shaking my head I say, Fuck this, and storm out the door. Stumbling on the gravel path, I text my wife, asking if everything is OK, but her *last seen* is two hours ago.

59

As the taxi drives at high speed over the elevated freeway, I look out the cruddy window. The silhouettes of buildings vanish in the cloud of smog like ghosts from a previous time, and down below, a few people walk out of the haze.

And the air is still disgusting, I say.

The driver nods in front of me and points a finger to his right. On clear days, you can see the volcanos.

He's mistaken me for a tourist, I figure, so I play to his error, and say, Wow, when does that happen?

Oh, never again, mi amigo, never again.

I lower the window to let a draft of air in. No matter how toxic, the car's speed might make it refreshing. This city, I say, not a catastrophe, nor a dystopia. It's just ill.

He nods and shrugs, letting go of the wheel for more time than I would like. But look ahead, he says, nada de tráfico, and he's right; as we soar down the road, the lanes ahead are completely empty.

When I'm dropped off outside my door, the city performs its best attempt at silence, a noisy silence—a staticky vacuum filled with the distant bark of dogs, the sweet potato vendor's whistle, but then by a deep, guttural call, *Gide, Lord Alfred*, the Famous-Armless-Writer's voice somewhere out of sight. I run inside my building to avoid him.

The walls of our bedroom are now completely covered in black ink, and the mock-up looks like a three-dimensional re-creation of the epic expressionist film *Metropolis*—only with more trees. My wife is sleeping faceup in bed, her hands meeting over her chest like a dead person laid out for their vigil. I run a firm hand over her forehead, and this sets off a series of movements on her face: a frown, a wrinkle across her forehead, her eyelids flickering. I try a soothing caress. Go back to sleep, I whisper and kiss her forehead.

Somewhere in the background, the Famous-Armless-Writer's muffled calls echo through the neighborhood. Then more barking, louder, right outside our window.

Make them shut up, my wife mumbles, her eyes still shut.

Sliding the window open, I find the pack of dogs I saw yesterday in the middle of Marsella Street. One of the Famous-Armless-Writer's dogs is wrestling a chunk of food from another, while others bark excitedly around them.

Then another, even more distant call, Gide, Lord Alfred, but the two mutts no longer respond to their names. From the right, the Would-Be-Writer enters my frame of vision and slows his pace. He stoops forward, in disbelief it seems, and tip toes closer to the pack. A few dogs turn to face him and bark, and one of them even has a run at him, forcing him to retreat at full speed. When the dog returns to face the battle within the pack, the Would-Be-Writer approaches again, Gide, Lord Alfred, he says, here boys, and he kneels a few feet from the pack. He tries coaxing them near with kissing noises, repeating *doggies* three times as he keeps moving closer—the threat of rabies clearly far from his mind. However, this movement earns him the attention of more dogs, Gide or Lord Alfred among them. When he is at arm's length of the dogs again, a few scatter while others begin barking at him, flashing their fangs; two have a go at his arms. He flails but not fast enough to avoid one of them biting his elbow. The Would-Be-Writer screams bloody murder, and the dog lets go of him, taking a piece of his shirt in his muzzle. His eyes widen at the sight of his torn sleeve, but it's not enough to scare him away; the promise of the book, of publication alongside the Famous-Armless-Writer, is too much of an incentive. Kneeling down in front of the pack again, he keeps whistling at the dogs, whispering, Gide, Lord Alfred. The fight for the piece of food has been forgotten, and now it appears the Would-Be-Writer's flesh is the true object of desire.

Behind me, my wife moans, What the fuck is happening out there?

Her complaints are not enough to make me turn to her or to slide the window shut.

The Would-Be-Writer taps the pavement with both his hands, Come here, now, he says in a childish, high-pitched voice, Here, now, Gide, Lord Alfred, and on that, another dog, a larger, wolf-like mutt, makes an openmouthed run at him and bites his hand. The Would-Be-Writer's roar is loud enough to attract the attention of a few neighbors peeking from their windows like me, Help, he yells, my dogs.

The Famous-Armless-Writer is still nowhere in sight, somehow not in range of the Would-Be-Writer's yelps, Help, somebody, please, but it's only him in the middle of the pack, the dogs closing in on him. When he sees there's no escape, he crawls in the direction of Gide and Lord Alfred, slowly, timidly, Here now, doggies, he whimpers, and in a brave dive, he throws himself over the dogs, tackles Gide and Lord Alfred, grabs them by their collars and hangs on. The other dogs scatter but then immediately converge on him. The wolf-like dog bites his hand again, Help, he yells, clutching Gide and Lord Alfred close while the rest of the pack growls and whines.

Only then does the rushing figure of the Famous-Armless-Writer reappear.

Gide, Lord Alfred, he says, where were you? And he kicks out and swings his hook at the rest of the dogs, all of which retreat to a safe distance.

With the affair settled, the neighbors return to their homes.

What's all that noise? my wife asks again, but I keep staring out, the only spectator left, alone, as Rimbaud once put it, in possessing a key to this barbarous sideshow.

60

Despite the recent clamor, El Harar is quiet, just a wet wind, then a shy drizzle darkening the vibrant red gravel and a swirl of blackening clouds overhead. No gun blasts, no ebbing trail of narcocorridos sounding behind the adobe wall. Time, in its revered circularity, seems to have come back around to the day that I returned to this place. As my brother opens the door, I'm expecting to see coffee beans and rice littering the floor.

When we step inside, though, the floor is sparkling and the scent all around us is the synthetic clean of an air freshener.

What do you think is going on? my brother says, not turning back to me, quickening his pace.

The living room is crepuscular behind my polarized sunglasses. The window is open, allowing the wet breeze into the room. On the leather couch, my mother is sitting next to the clairvoyant, both of them dressed in white linen tunics and opal necklaces.

Just seeing my mother on the couch lends the scene a dreamlike quality; her favorite lounger is empty, throbbing almost, a few feet to her side.

My brother stoops down to kiss my mother on both cheeks, then completely ignores the clairvoyant. My mother shakes her head lightly but then opens a palm that shows my brother to her chair. Alex, she says, sit there.

Doubtful, he looks over to me as if I should offer confirmation or challenge his position as the heir, but seeing that I have no objection, he lowers his body onto the chair.

I remain standing at the other end of the room. What is all this? I say, trying to eye both my mother and the clairvoyant at once.

The clairvoyant turns to my mother and gives her a single nod.

This cannot longer wait, my mother says, looking vaguely out the window.

To me, it seems like the clairvoyant is behind these words, that my mother's pensive yet vacant stare is that of a ventriloquist's dummy.

The time has come . . .

The clairvoyant hunkers forward, grips my mother's hands, and coaxes her on.

The curse has fallen, my mother says, then swallows.

My brother holds the armrests of my mother's lounger like an airplane passenger during turbulence. I look down, my thumb and index finger tight on my temples. Shaking my head mildly, I say, Curse, always with this curse—

Shut up, my mother cuts in, and the clairvoyant comes to her defense.

Yes, shut up and listen to what your mother has to say, she tells me, her eyes shifting to a defiant dart. A cold feeling washes over my chest. Breathing in, I turn to my brother, whose posture is so tense it seems like he might break a bone.

I have cancer, my mother says, and the cold inside me begins to swell, grazing my every organ. My brother goes white, and the clairvoyant lays a palm over my mother's back, squeezes her shoulder.

It's breast cancer, my mother says, not as early a stage as we might want.

For several long seconds, the only sound is the patter of the rain, sure and steady on the skylight.

If and when the time comes, she adds, opening her purse and pulling out her gold-plated handgun, I want half my ashes shot out of this pistol, skyward. She places the handgun on the couch and fetches something else from her purse. The other half, I want stored in here, and she pulls out a metallic urn in the shape of a bullet, uncapping it to show us the empty insides. Even in the distance, I can make out "Alex" engraved in the silvery surface of the urn. A knot grows in my throat, threatening to burst.

My brother remains rigid on the lounger, empty of words, while the clairvoyant squeezes my mother's hands tightly, holding her gaze.

A decision must be made soon, my mother says.

My brother and I nod in unison.

We must decide, my mother says, *as a family*, if we want to carry on.

My brother seems on the verge of talking but keeps gripping the chair. The rain continues; my mother turns to my brother.

Alex, she says, that chair is yours if you want it. You've worked for it.

Bathed in a sudden beam of clear light from the skylight, as if the sun had been saving all its might and maneuvered past the clouds just for this declaration, my brother turns to me with an expression that resembles the clairvoyant's: victorious and certain.

In that moment, as I'm looking at his grotesque smile, it seems like the tightly woven threads of my existence are beginning to loosen. I turn away and storm out the door, deep into the rain, and release the knot in my throat.

The tears in my eyes make the world a blur, but I manage to walk past El Harar's wall and stare towards the distant haze, where the pollution over the city renders the sunset a yellow reminiscent of rotten fruit.

61

During the ride back home, my moods shift wildly between rage, confusion, and despair. Arriving at our door, my skin feverish, my heart racing, the only thing driving me forward is the promise of being held in my wife's arms.

The image that keeps coming to me is that of my mother when she was pregnant with me, sitting in her lounger, running a hand over her belly like my wife does these days. All this time, while wishing for the end of the gun business, I hadn't really understood that the end of it could only come with the end of her.

Climbing the stairs to our bedroom, my stride weak and heavy, I notice an array of blue Post-its pasted over the scribbles on the walls. Every inch of drywall is covered with my wife's spidery handwriting, and over every formula, the stickers hold abstractions of language, headers and bullet points that might elucidate the numbers, *The Fifth Sun: Contemporary Apocalypse,* or *Ciudad Moctezuma: Unsustainable Water Treatment,* or *Paseo de la Malinche: Ecological Treason.*

She is asleep again, faceup, completely still. I tiptoe up to the bed and lie next to her, watching the rise and fall of her chest, placing my hand gently over our daughter.

I get the urge to wake her up just for company, to tell her about the fulfillment of the curse. The silence is shattered by the loud buzz of my cellphone, and my wife frowns and squirms. A message from the Would-Be-Writer: *we are waiting for you, final meeting, remember?*

62

Despite the ban on one-fifth of the city's cars, there is still rush hour traffic on the streets. The endless demonstrations on Bucareli Avenue block this key vein, causing bottlenecks and jams. Protestors cover the area to decry the rising price of tortillas, the power outages, and the water shortages; they are joined by ecologists demanding a ban on adulterated gasoline, women drawing pink crosses on national emblems and statues due to the rise in femicides, farmers marching naked for the restitution of their land, and parents searching for their lost children. All of them competing for the attention of the secretary of state, who is tucked safely inside the government building with the dead-still tricolored flag above it.

In the distance, the ochre sunset has turned black, and the smells of human piss and busted plumbing follow me as I cut through the throngs leading to Café La Habana, the spot the Would-Be-Writer picked for our final meeting.

When I get to the café, I remove my sunglasses and stare at my reflection in the window and find that my pterygium is now masking half of my eye, lending the inner half a fleshy whiteness cut with blood-red veins. Behind my darkened reflection, I can see the literary trio—the Would-Be-Writer, the Famous-Armless-Writer, the American-Faux-Stridentist, and the two dogs chained to the legs of their table.

Entering, I'm greeted by a vampire-like host with a balding head full of freckles. Beside him, there's a plaque honoring Roberto Bolaño and Che Guevara, two of the café's regular customers back in its glory days, having been the place where both *The Savage Detectives* and the Cuban Revolution were plotted.

He leads me in, and I offer handshakes around the table. I can't avoid a smirk when I spot the Would-Be-Writer's left arm wrapped in a bandage. Luckily, my chair is farthest from the dogs, who whine restlessly next to their owner.

Sitting down, the weight of my mother's news is still heavy in my mind, and I know I must have a look so lost, a face so dead, that perhaps it is hard for those around me to see me, to feel my presence.

The noise from the protests outside pours its muffled sounds into the café, mixing with the hiss of steamers and rattle of cups, creating a maddening roar inside it.

Why did you pick this most convenient place? I ask.

The Would-Be-Writer looks up at me with what might be contempt, but because of my obscured sight, I can't really make out the subtleties of gesture.

History was made here, he says.

Una ícono literario, the American-Faux-Stridentist joins in.

As I wince and nod, the Famous-Armless-Writer steps to their defense and says, The place gives them a literary high.

Is that not normal? the Would-Be-Writer asks, eyeing us all, then pulling out the final proof of their book from his backpack after the lack of a response. The dogs beside him growl at his every move, and it takes a shush from the Famous-Armless-Writer and a pull on their collars to calm them.

A round of knee-rattling doppios arrives as I add my final suggestions to their document, offering brief, self-explanatory sentences with every mark of the pen.

They all nod as they look at my right eye, which I think they enjoy watching, as if the pterygium itself could suck in all the impurities from their texts, gathering them all in the form of its red, burst veins. They continue to nod with the urgency of it all wrapping up: the text, our meetings, this evening.

Luckily, we finish editing before the height of the drunken bedlam rises, before the mariachi band that trudged all the way from Plaza Garibaldi begins its deadly "Jarabe Tapatío," the tune played loud enough to make the Famous-Armless-Writer's dogs' barks rise to a frenzy.

Handing me the last of my payments, the Famous-Armless-Writer excuses himself and takes his furious canines outside. The

American-Faux-Stridentist shakes my hand, says, Chingón, gracias, adding a tap on my shoulder, and follows the Famous-Armless-Writer outside, lighting a cigarette before he exits the premises. Outside, he pets the dogs while taking a drag, the cigarette's tip burning orange, then dying out.

Left behind with the Would-Be-Writer, I watch him take good care at fitting the final proof into his backpack, making sure every page is in its place.

What's with you? he asks. Seems like you're somewhere else.

I shake my head, What happened to your hand?

He looks at the bandage, Dog bite, believe it or not.

Yeah, kinda heard.

It seems like my comment throws him off. What? He winces. Who told you?

Can't really remember.

OK, look. He stands. Gotta go. See you at the launch, yes?

I didn't see my credit in there, I say, pointing at the manuscript.

Don't worry. I'll add the colophon as soon as I get home.

Yeah, you do that, I say, looking off into the café, which is packed with anonymous diners. It seems way too easy to be effaced from the world these days.

63

The following morning, the pediatrician shows up at our duplex with what you might call British timeliness. His initial and emphatic *Nice place* soon shifts. With a fearful stare, his wide eyes dart from the scribbled-on walls with blue Post-its to my eye, which is now bisected by the veiny flesh of my pterygium. You people *do* live a creative lifestyle, he says. Turning to me, he adds, And you have half an eye now! His sight then lingers on my wife's mock-up and the dog-eared copy of *La Leyenda de los Soles* beside it. She has narrowed down the working titles of her project to two: *Paseo de la Malinche* and *La Posible Realidad del Quinto Sol*.

This morning, she's complaining about a stinging sensation in her lower back. It comes in waves, and I can't tell if it's icy or burning, she says through a frown, rubbing her hand over the offending area, but for a long moment, the pediatrician continues to stare at her mock-up.

What's all this? he asks, making a circular motion with his index finger over the projected slice of Reforma.

She's an urban planner, I say, turning to my wife, who only purses her lips in pain. This was the project she put forth to complete during her maternity leave. She's been designing this for more than eight months now.

The pediatrician nods, looking over the clutter of papier-mâché trees, index finger now resting on his chin, not really making an effort to listen to what I'm saying, so I just join him in staring at the complexity of my wife's imagined world. When this pregnancy is over, she will dress up in her work clothes again and present this before the board at her office, this plan for an ideal city, an ideal stretch of it, at least, a microcosm of what it could become. But whether this plan will be carried out remains in doubt. It is only potential, after all, *The Possible Reality of the Fifth Sun*—like my life writing poems.

OK, enough of that, the pediatrician says, cutting my musings short, and walks around our bed to take my wife's pressure. Higher stakes here, right?

My wife cringes as he tightens the pressure gauge around her arm. Easy, she says, tender skin, but he carries on without real care. Come here, my wife demands, extending a hand.

Pressure's still high, the pediatrician says. That's what's causing the pain. He unzips his white backpack and pulls out his laptop with an ultrasound probe hooked to it. After spreading the cold gel on my wife's belly, the image shows our daughter in her sitting position, and the sight of her sends a choking sensation down my throat. My wife notices and squeezes my hand.

So, chances are she won't be turning. You're having one steadfast daughter, the pediatrician says, trying for laughs but utterly failing. After a light pause and a clearing of his throat, he adds, We'll give her a few more days, but if your blood pressure doesn't recede, we're pulling her out; we can't take any risks.

We look at him as if expecting more words, some of them redeeming, perhaps, but he only packs his things into his backpack, zips it up, and flings it over one shoulder.

Your nurse will move in with you until your baby is delivered, he says, to which my wife just nods.

As I'm leading him downstairs, he can't seem to take his sight from my eye.

What? I ask, holding the door open for him.

Nothing, he says, before heading out. Nothing at all.

64

Having made our nurse feel as at home as possible in our barely furnished lower story, I leave for El Harar. Crossing the gates, I notice that the National Guard members allegedly looking out for us have diminished in numbers, almost by the day, to the point where there are only two of them left, our family guns hanging limply from bands around their shoulders and two crumpled bags of Doritos in each set of their spice-dusted hands.

Past my former Bronco, now decrepit and covered with watermarks, I head for the office, where the mood is already funereal albeit still reeking of air freshener. My mother's huge office is empty, the desk is gone, and the armoires with collectible guns have been moved to my brother's office—as though the belongings of a dead person have already made way for what comes next in the land of the living.

Breathless, I make my way to the living room, where there is complete silence: no rain landing on the skylight and the disconnected telephone at my brother's feet. He naps in my mother's— now *his*—lounger, wearing the same suit he had on when my mother broke the news. The urn with his name and hers is sitting beside him on the rug. On my desk there's a note in my mother's handwriting, something like a mediocre couplet of a poem, as if she was looking for a poignant way of communicating with me, No Need to be Glum / Pressing Work to Get Done. I toss it into my drawer and slam it shut.

Behind me, startled, my brother wakes from his slouching position.

Is that where you'll sleep now? Moving permanently to El Harar, are you?

He rubs his eyes, What? You scared me.

New king trying out his throne?

He yawns, allowing himself a few seconds to gain full lucidity. Not the time to be jealous.

Jealous? Are you kidding? All I want is out, away from this.

Decide what you must. I don't want anyone here who isn't committed to working for me.

Listen to yourself. You've buried her already.

Do you see her around?

That's sick, Alex.

Shaking his head lightly, he picks up the bullet-shaped urn, runs his fingers over his engraved name.

Is that where *you* want your ashes too? Your name's already on it.

He keeps on staring, as if reading his own name poses some sort of difficulty. Still holding the urn, he turns to me. What do you think it means?

What does *what* mean, Alex?

That she gave me her name.

For one, it means we never had a father, remember?

He shakes his head and rolls his eyes. What I mean is, why did she give *me* the same name and not *you*? You're the firstborn, after all.

Go ask the clairvoyant. Draw some cards.

OK, be that way, then.

I'm here to work, not to serve as your in-house therapist.

Here to work, then, are you? That's a first.

Yeah, I say, looking through my desk for the ammunition order. Where is it? I ask, walking to him, my shadow looming over him.

Where's *what*?

The order, I say, turning and walking into his office to find it on his desk, a dry coffee ring printed over the letters on the first page.

Coming back out with it, I shake the sheets of paper in front of him. Don't you dare! This is my order to approve, not yours.

He stands and lazily walks to grab a blanket from the couch and sits back on the lounger. Whatever, he says, turning his back to me, shutting his eyes.

Slamming the door of my office, order in hand, I go through the books to see if there is any precedent like this, but it seems that my mother has always covered her trails—invoices, even if they are fake, match every single shipment and sale, and all of them are signed by our gallant friend, the secretary of defense. How many collectibles and liters of Cognac did it take? Signing off on this would mean agreeing to the shadiest deal to date, not to mention spurring on the threats posed by that hoarse voice on behalf of that cartel.

My eyes are sore after staring at the small print of every invoice in the feeble light of my office. I rest my head on the desk, letting my eyelids flutter, thinking of my daughter, of how this deal could financially secure the first years of her life. The pragmatic thoughts soon begin to bend, though. As the eye flutters become longer and more pronounced, the images in my head begin to slant places, people, situations, transporting me somewhere that bears no resemblance to any place I know but that I nonetheless understand as the cemetery where my mother's family's remains are stored inside a crypt. My brother, my mother, and I are sitting on tombs greened with moss, and we are waiting, staring ahead at the crematorium, over which a chimney crown is expelling gray smoke, the remnants of who, I don't know. I'm staring at the smoke without feeling any fear or grief even though my wife and daughter are not there with me, and as we stare, a loud tapping sound begins behind us, but I'm the only one to turn, and as the hollow sound continues, my eyelids jerk, in the dream it seems, at first, then their flutter gives way to the knots on the wooden surface of my desk. Another bang makes the scene fade out, and I realize someone is pounding loudly on my office door. My mouth like cotton gauze, I get up and undo the lock, and as soon as I do, my brother pushes through, Get your ass out here, he says—a commotion too sudden compared to the quiet sequence of my dream. He pushes me out of my office to look out the window of the living room, where, behind the Ford Bronco, a thick tower of dark smoke rises inside El Harar's walls. What happens next seems too surreal to be true: a large chunk of wood engulfed in flames flies over the wall, landing inside the property, setting the taller stalks of grass near the perimeter on fire.

They want us to burn, my brother barks, loading his gun with a new cartridge.

Are you planning on extinguishing those flames by shooting them?

This is an attack, you idiot.

I stumble towards the storage room to find the fire extinguishers, and as I return to the living room with them, I see the National Guard bodyguards tossing water from a large bucket onto the flames, which makes them disappear at first, but it's not nearly enough; the flames blaze on, livid.

My brother then appears outside too, shooting skyward, as if our mother's ashes were already inside that gun.

When I catch up with the guards, I stare upward, wondering where the usual afternoon downpour is, and find only a gray sky more akin to the city's; the pieces of wood continue to smoke and burn as our bodyguards toss more water onto them, but then, another large, burning log is hurled our way, flung well over the wall and reeking of burnt gasoline. Its bark is blazing red and snapping. It rolls our way and slams against one of our bodyguard's legs, knocking him over. My brother unloads the rest of his cartridge in a fit of rage, but the flames are starting to catch more leaves and grass, so I let the foam from the extinguisher spray loose. At the same time, the remaining bodyguard empties his water bucket onto the log. The doused log hisses like the frying oil at a food stall. The rush of smoke envelopes us, burning my eyes with an acid sting. I toss the extinguisher aside and fall to my knees, sticking my hands over both my eyes, screaming. I can hear the extinguisher still going off, but all I can smell is burnt wood. Lying on the ground, my eyes clenched shut, I make out my brother's voice calling on the bodyguards to carry me back to the house. The sight behind my lids is dark with spots of red.

After placing me on the couch, they pour water over my face, into my open eyes, but I keep on screaming out in pain. In the background, there's a scratchy voice from the bodyguards' radios. They plead for backup; my brother connects the telephone line and does the same. Soon, police and firefighter sirens wail in the distance.

After some minutes, I lift myself from the couch, feeling my way to the bathroom. My brother catches up, holds me for balance, and guides me inside, where I place my face under the running tap, letting more water flow into my eyes. Mustering the courage to open them, my brother jolts back, terrified, Fuck's sake! Can you see out of that eye?

He points to the mirror with a shaking finger, and the glassy surface reveals that while my left eye is bloodshot and swollen, lined with black coal marks on its lids, my right eye has been taken over by my pterygium, rendering it completely white with red spots of pooled blood in it. My pupil, my green iris, are a mere shadow behind what looks like the white of a fried egg.

65

The following morning, I wake up to a stream of blood oozing from my right eye. The dampness on my pillow pulled me from a dream where there was no fleshy, bloody eye, my daughter had been safely delivered, and my wife's mock-up was being erected along Reforma. Running a hand over my cheek, which is sticky with blood, I scream out and wake my wife, who squirms at the sight of red stains on my pillow and our covers, My baby! she screams, My daughter! Everything in front of me is a collection of floating distortions, and it's hard to tell one thing from the next. Even so, I try soothing her, No, no, she's fine. It's me, I say, pressing a firm thumb over the lachrymal gland of my right eye, where the blood seems to be pouring from. She turns to me, moves my thumb aside, and watches the stream of blood leaking from my ghostly eye, which sends her into a fit of sobs, What happened to it? she wails. The commotion has called the attention of the nurse who, in her white sleeping robe and hair curlers, arrives at our second-story bedroom, medical kit in hand. Disoriented by the sight of blood on the covers, her first concern is my wife. She checks her vital symptoms, searching for blood between her legs, but my wife keeps saying, It's him. It's his eye. The nurse, with spread-open hands, replies, OK, OK, but you need to calm down. Do it for your baby. After that, she makes me lie flat on the bed and says the best thing she can do for me is add a dab of Vaseline on the corner of my eye before sending me to my ophthalmologist with a hand towel pressed to the wound.

The red-haired ophthalmologist is not in when I get to her office, but her associate is. She makes me wait to the wide-eyed stares and averted eyes of every other patient there, my hand towel soaking red. When she allows me inside the office, she stands firm behind an invisible wall of pride. Let's see what we have here, she says, stoic, laying me down and pouring eye drops into my bad eye. She asks me to shut both my eyes. When everything is pitch black, she says, Talk about a white and bloody eye, eh? Next thing you know, it'll be made out of glass. You should've let me work on it when we had the chance. Trying to keep calm, I tell her, I'm sure I heard the word *benign* quite clearly from your associate's mouth. She dabs more Vaseline on my eye and says, You won't die from it. Then why is it bleeding? I almost scared my pregnant wife to death this morning. She pulls back, Oh, one would think you'd scare her on a daily basis like this, and not only your wife. Why is there blood? I ask again. In a voice not even feigning patience, she responds, I don't know, and finishes her procedure with the sting of a syringe in the inner edge of my eye. The pain is so sharp, so sudden and cringe-inducing, that it makes me dizzy. My sight seems to fade, and my consciousness is suddenly flooded by white light.

66

When I come to, I have tiny pieces of alcohol-soaked gauze stuck in my nostrils. It takes me a moment to understand where I am—the intense pool of light around me, the whiteness of the room, the smell of sterilization, the equipment rattling on the doctor's metallic tray, her pupils fixed on me like black pearls. Awake again? she says. I sure hope so, I say, my blinks long and tight. Approaching me, she says, Might I finish the procedure now? I nod, my open eyes catching rotating blobs of light. She performs a slight suture of my lachrymal, and all the while, the white light comes rushing in. That light, I tell her, I thought I was dying, that I was coming out of the tunnel. She doesn't respond, just leans back, and says, All done, off you go. Like this? Don't you have a patch or something? No, she says, leading me out the door. Now if you don't mind, I have to tend to my *scheduled* appointments.

Walking out of the building and into the midday haze, every object, close and far, seems to be merging with the next.

67

The world shifts surreally in front of me as I text my wife, *Everything fine now, no blood.*

Why is it all white and bloody? Can you see out of it?

Reading her message, it seems like my depth perception has been tweaked, and covering the bad eye doesn't readjust it. I text back, *I can see, yes ... how are you?*

Scared.

And our baby? What does the nurse say?

No changes there. High blood pressure. Says I need to calm down.

Calm down then, everything's fine here too.

But why was it ALL WHITE AND BLOODY?

We'll deal with it soon. Zero danger. I'll see you in a bit.

The visit with the doctor has eaten up a good part of the day, so I take off to El Harar. The pain around my eyelids is sharp, and there is a steady pulse at the core of my bad eye. I ride with my eyes shut behind my sunglasses. When my taxi drops me off, I have to readjust to the day's glare even behind my polarized lenses. On the adobe walls of the property, there seems to be a spray-painted legend, which I can't really make out. Approaching the guards, I ask them to read it out to me. One of them goes near the vandalized wall and, after gulping down some Coca-Cola, reads the words, marking every syllable: *Complete that order and this is just the start.* I have to repeat the sentence in my mind to make sense of it, and immediately, there is a tremor in my chest. Crossing El Harar's gates, the air sharp in my lungs, I walk by the logs and stare at their burnt, black bark and the patches of dead grass.

Inside the house, there's that smell of old coffee again. Fuck, no, please, I catch myself blurting out and find that my mother's former office is now arranged like a bedroom—a king-sized bed taking over the space once occupied by her desk. Looking down, I find the trail of coffee and rice from the front door to the foot of her bed. Fighting off the urge to recoil, I slam the door shut behind me and find my brother sleeping on the lounger again, oozing a scent of putrid fruit. Approaching him, I stumble over the bullet-shaped urn and a nearly empty bottle of that high-end Cognac at his feet. The suit he is wearing looks like the same one he wore yesterday and the day before that. I head to my office; the ammunition order is nowhere to be found. I fumble through the drawers, feeling for any sheet of paper but find only the splinters in the wood. A cold feeling settles in my gut, and I only realize I'm hurrying in my brother's direction when I hear the loud shuffling of my feet. I shake him awake by the shoulders, the scent of smoke lifting from his disheveled hair. As his eyelids flick open, he screams out, like my wife did at the sight of my bad eye. What the fuck? he screams, but I keep on shaking him. *What the fuck?* I say, What the fuck is wrong with *you?* Are you drunk? His eyes dart about, No, he says, wiping his mouth. He shoots a look at the bottle at his feet, OK, he concedes, but then quiets, allowing me to yell straight into his ear, Why are you going into my office? Where's that order? The mention of it bathes him in lucidity, Oh,

I approved it, he says, slouching back into his usual smugness. The wire has already come in. We don't have your abundant time around here. Like when I was putting the fire out, a flood of heat comes over my face. You did what? I ask him, shaking him by his shoulders again. Where's Mother? He pushes my hands away, Not here. I circle the room with my hands on my head. Does she know? I ask him, staring straight at him while he calmly lounges on his new chair. He clears his throat, then says, I don't think she wants to anymore. His nonchalant voice makes me scream at him even louder, Did you even see the sign outside? He goes quiet for a second and looks out the window, What sign? he says, returning his blank stare to me, oblivious. OK, I say, turning away. Sounds like you've signed another death sentence. He rolls his eyes, You've gone mad, you know that? Just look at yourself, that fucking eye. I head in the direction of the door, Take this exchange as my resignation, I tell him and walk out, glancing at the sky, where the sun, shining through the clouds, spills its white light over my face.

68

Back home, I meet my wife and the nurse in our second-story bedroom while they share a pot of bougainvillea tea. After drinking a sip, my wife sets the cup aside and asks me to sit next to her. When we are face to face, she lifts my sunglasses. I can tell she is fighting off the fear and the disgust, but she only slants her brows to convey tenderness. What happened? she says, running her warm thumbs along my cheekbones. Long story. I'll tell you all about it sometime, I say, leaning my head on the soft spot of her neck. She clicks her tongue and shakes her head, then says, My very own *enfant terrible*. I breathe out slowly, the air from my nostrils hot, then run a hand over her belly, Let's just focus on *her* for now, get her to us. My wife nods to this, and it seems like the nurse does too, And then, we are taking care of that eye for good. I nod too, and so does the nurse, more vehemently this time. On that, my wife jerks back, Oh, she says, *this* came for you. She reaches over the bedside and hands me a hardcover book with an orange cover, Valery's book, she says with a smirk. *Valery*? I ask. Holding the book, turning it over, and getting close with my left eye, I can make out the image of a fallen tree branch over the orange backdrop. You know, she says, your very own Paul Valery. Only then do I realize: this is it—the book authored by the Would-Be-Writer, the Famous-Armless-Writer, and the American-Faux-Stridentist. Flipping through the pages, looking for the colophon, for my name in the shifting and blurring letters, past a page with their bios and pictures, where even the two hideous dogs are featured, it is nowhere to be found. The fucking asshole, I say, shutting the book and tossing it back over the bedside. What? my wife says while the nurse widens her eyes and places a palm on her chest. Long story too, I say, grabbing a cup and pouring myself some of the pink, soothing tea. I have a sip, then say, But the villain in this one won't get away with it.

69

The first raindrops fall sporadically, splatting on the gravel; some are lost and inaudible, falling on the burnt stalks of grass or on the roof of the house. They are clear beads in the incipient light of the afternoon. My mother's footsteps crunch slowly and heavily over the gravel, and mine too are cumbersome as seeing from only one eye renders the world a spatial trap. Her first chemo session has depleted her, and she has to weakly grip my forearm as she walks. She stares out in the direction of the city before reaching the door, her eyelids probably carrying memories of the spectacular sunsets of her youth, the times when we had healthier skies, That brown cloak of smog, she says, what ever happened to our opalescent twilights? I've long forgotten them too, I tell her, as if I knew what those sunsets looked like. We step onto the portico just as the rain begins to quicken.

Inside, we walk past the leather lounger with my brother's blanket on it and the empty bottle of Cognac on the rug. Inside her room, I tuck her in bed. Once on the soft incline of her pillow, she places a hand over mine, Take off your sunglasses, son, and when I do, she gives me a pained laugh and a strained shake of the head. You look like a horror movie, she says, then pauses and looks away from me. Your brother said you're no longer part of the business. Her smile is feeble, her blinks slow. That's a new record, only thirteen days on the job. One might think you're lazy and weak. Kicking at the coffee and rice on the floor, I say, What matters now is that you get better. She squeezes my hand limply and says, I won't do this again, this whole chemo thing. The words trigger a hollowness in my chest, which she seems to spot in my face right away. I don't have that kind of fight in me anymore. I'm doing the mastectomy, and if that doesn't work, I'll remain at the sickness's hands. I give her a slow nod, resigned, and as she sinks deeper into the softness of her pillow, a gunshot goes off somewhere on the grounds, then a second, and third in quick succession. While I get an immediate pang of nerves like lightning all over my body, it only makes my mother's eyes shoot up in desperation. That's your brother, and that's my gun, she says. Please tell him to calm down and sober up on your way out.

I nod and kiss her forehead, catching sight of the dark gray in the roots of her hair.

Walking out into the rain, my brother is nowhere in sight, and there are no more gun blasts. I look for him without success and then walk to the bus stop. Every passing minute has me looking at the clock on my phone, hoping I'll make it to the Would-Be-Writer's reading in time despite still not knowing how I'll intervene, if I'll even be brave enough to let everyone there know I'm the ghostwriter behind his text. As the bus rumbles my way, my phone vibrates in my pocket. My mother's voice streams from it when I answer, her voice loud and irked, It's your brother, she says. He's drunk again, carrying around my gun. Please come back. I can't deal with this shit right now. I hang up and stare in the direction of the valley, where the cloud of smog above the city seems to tear for a second, revealing a suggestion of a pale, white sun, washing weakly over the buildings in the distance.

70

As I step back inside the gates, I hear a shot, and a bullet slices through the leaves of the taller trees inside the property. My brother comes into my blurred line of sight, stumbling around the house, and unleashes another blast that bounces off the Ford Bronco with a metallic din. My body goes cold, and my breath quickens. I seek refuge behind the car. Alex, I yell out, have you fucking gone mad? The only response I get is the shy rain falling over the land. I'm coming out, I yell. Do not shoot your brother, and I peek over the Bronco's hood, raising my arms. The rain distorts the scenery ahead and gives the impression that he is lost in some faraway distance. My mother's gun hangs from one hand, while with the other he manages to grip both a newly opened bottled of Cognac and the bullet-shaped urn, a blanket swaddled over his shoulders. I try approaching him, stooping and hands upraised, What's this shit about? I tell him, but instead of looking my way, he takes a long gulp of Cognac, What in hell is wrong with you? I yell, and as he unplugs the bottle from his mouth, a stream of liquor dribbling down his chin, he turns to me and coughs, Gave me her name, and now she is going to die, he says with a pronounced slur, and for a second, it sounds as though the mad heir wants to do in the queen. Is that what this is about, your goddam name? I let my arms fall to my sides and quote Rimbaud at him, *O mother, I'm the slave of my baptism, you have caused my misfortune and you have caused your own!* He doesn't respond to this, rather takes another swig from his bottle. After swallowing with a frown, he says, She's done everything for us and this business, but *you* can't see it. Thinking him harmless, my body loosens, and I walk quickly towards him, sure that he is sufficiently lucid not to fire a bullet in my direction, but, in a sudden movement, he raises the gun, dropping the bottle and urn to the ground. The urn rolls away slowly, and his focus settles on putting me in his crosshairs. His arms stretch forward, trembling, he says, Maybe you and I should die. We're so useless. We're destroying the tower. All my muscles taut, I begin a slow retreat, my hands stiff above my shoulders again, Listen to this nonsense, I tell him with a cracked voice. You're shit-faced. He lowers the gun at this and stares at the ground. Reaching for the bottle and the urn a few feet ahead of him, his movements are slow and clumsy, frail even. A window of opportunity slides open, and even though a heavy heartbeat pulses inside me, I sprint forward and throw myself at him, and as I tackle him to the ground, the gun goes off. Its loud, ear-piercing blast rises above every other sound, brightening the scenery, making it spin around me with a jagged dazzle until everything goes white.

71

I blink. I can barely make out the dark red of the wet gravel and my shattered sunglasses beside me. A few feet to my other side, my brother groans like a netherworld creature. Family bullet? Friendly fire? My wrist throbs as if it has a heartbeat of its own, and I can picture the blood spewing from it, pooling over the gravel, staining the burnt grass. A few seconds of stillness go by, with only the din of the rain around us. My brother keeps on gasping in pain, which seems like good news, a sign of life, but I try to keep a close eye on him as he flails his arms in the direction of the gun, which lies next to the urn on the soaked ground. I crawl over, grabbing the gun and tossing it farther away from him, and then kneel on the gravel, holding what might be a wound on my left wrist. As I apply pressure to it, the door to the house flings open, and my mother emerges, her eyes tired, angry. Catching sight of the bottle of Cognac, my shattered sunglasses, her gun and urn glimmering on the gravel, and my semi-conscious brother at her foot, she says, The stupid children I reared. With slow steps, she recovers her urn and gun and then kneels beside me, lifting my wounded wrist to her face. He only grazed you, she says, rubbing my hand all the way to the fish-hooked life line on my palm. Be thankful you're whole. She lets go of my hand and walks back inside, stopping at the door. Bring that sack of idiocy inside, she tells me, giving a backward nod in the direction of my brother. I eventually lift and drag him into my office, locking the door behind me. I head out after that, straight for the Ford Bronco this time, sure I'll find the keys hanging from the ignition. The engine whines like an injured horse, but it lets me drive the car out of the gates and towards the city, where the heavy pollution dresses the valley in an ashy dusk in which the dimming light seems to float.

72

Darkness pours over the valley. Behind the wheel of the Bronco, I soon realize this partial blindness is not what I expected. It's less of a blur now, rather a chiaroscuro, a world made up of shadows, making it difficult to drive. After a few scares in the final descent of the highway, all of them due to my treacherous perception of depth, I decide to park the Bronco and carry on in a cab. At 7:00 p.m.—the hour when the transit system collapses, the hour where the roads are congested and nothing more than a trap, and when distances cease to be a meaningful expression of time—I'm already running half an hour late to the book launch. How long you think this will take? I ask the driver, trying to show only half my face in the rearview and holding my burning and throbbing wrist, which I keep veiled under the long sleeve of my jacket. He stares ahead at the red glare of brake lights and says, Hard to tell, hour or so. I shake my head and breathe out, Hell, I'm in a real hurry. He turns his head halfway and gives me a sarcastic, coughing laugh, Don't worry, caballero, time in this country. He pauses, raps his finger against the wheel. In this country, urgent messages arrive way after you expect them; the notes telling us a relative is sick arrive long after they've been buried. That's why foreigners think we are nothing but ghosts. I want to tell him he's been reading too much Rulfo but only say, I thought there was a ban on cars, to which he faintly nods, Rule of law, you say? Good example of how long that lasts 'round these parts. He slouches back on his seat; I strive for patience. Reaching out with his right hand, he cranks up the volume of his radio, from which an alarmed voice is reporting a slight eruption from the Popocatépetl Volcano, explaining that a rain of ash is to be expected in the city as far as Azcapotzalco. The driver whistles long and sour, Our invisible volcano, he says. Could no longer home what it held inside. He shakes his head, hisses, Mountains pregnant with destruction. A sharp pang goes off in my sternum, but I decide against responding to avoid a rhetorical crescendo. We both keep staring ahead at the thick funnel of cars dripping into the central areas of the city. A few miles down, I decide to continue on foot. I hand him a bill and linger beside the open door waiting for my change; he plays dumb for as long as he can. Change, sir? I ask him. Fishing for coins in his trouser pocket, he lowers his window, then lights a cigarette and exhales a dense fog of smoke through which his cupped palm cuts through to hand me my money.

During the walk down Reforma, along the edge of the city's largest park, my thoughts take on the shape of a maelstrom— why did the Would-Be-Writer neglect to add my credit? Was it intentional or ego-fueled forgetfulness? I'm also nervous, as I have nothing in mind to exact my revenge. Will I crash the reading? Walk up to the front of the room, take the microphone from his hand, spill it out to the crowd? Probably not. But perhaps my presence, standing tall at the back of the gathering, eyes fixed on the readers, will earn me some appreciation or recognition, a public apology, the Would-Be-Writer's embarrassed stares, at least. The final stretch towards the Museum of Modern Art has the first motes of ash falling from the sky, clear against the traffic's headlights and soon visible under my trailing footprints. At the gates of the museum, a large billboard announces the forthcoming exhibition, themed around the dystopian views of the muralist greats. The title reads *Anahuac: An Apocalyptic Vision of Pollution*, and the backdrop is a famous painting by Siqueiros, an expressionist rendering of our ozone-filled skies, an image not unlike the one around me now: the black sky plummeting on the city.

Once I'm there, behind the shadowy reflections of the glass doors of the museum, I can spot the three writers sitting beside each other, the audience pensively looking their way. Next to the reading table, the two dogs are chained to the Famous-Armless-Writer's chair. The American-Faux-Stridentist's mouth is already in motion. Looking in, ash starting to gather on my hair and my shoulders, my phone comes alive in a fit of pings and shooting lights. I reach into my trouser pocket and press the button to decline. Through the doors, their shadows and their glare, the Would-Be-Writer lifts his eyes and spots me looking in. He looks down at the table quickly and starts leafing through his book. When the American-Faux-Stridentist finishes reading and looks up towards the crowd, adding a sort of sitting bow, the muffled ripple of applause offers a window of opportunity for me to step in without interrupting, but as I place my palms on the cool glass door, I feel my phone vibrating again, its screen shining through the fabric of my pants.

I pull it out, see it's my wife calling, and decline, but another call comes in right away. Inside, the Would-Be-Writer is getting ready to read. He uncaps a water bottle and wets his lips with it, swishes a sip. My phone goes off again. I answer. Everything all right? I whisper. A second of silence, then, Arthur . . . I keep looking in to where the Would-Be-Writer is now closely monitoring me. Arthur, listen . . . I hear her words, a sound like all the others in the vicinity, a sound that is there but one that I'm filtering out, all too focused, even through this hazy sight, at what is happening inside. What's going on? Are you OK? And then another small silence. Her voice returns weak on the other end, No. My water broke. She's coming. *Now.* Get here. We'll be on our way to the hospital soon. The call ends with a beeping sound while, inside the museum, the Would-Be-Writer begins reading from his open book. Outside, deep in a sea of ash, the texture of reality seems to shatter, and unable to tell if the warm feeling coming over me is a rush of dopamine or an encroaching fear, I tap the glass doors of the museum, earning myself a choreographed turn of the audiences' necks. The Would-Be-Writer pauses, looks up in fear, but then I'm gone, ghostly, dashing away under the inevitable descent of our sky.

73

A thick layer of ash has gathered on the streets, and right outside our building, government workers are trimming the branches of the trees growing invasively into balconies and terraces. Their chainsaws let out an unebbing wave of noise, which is faintly muffled as I step inside our building. My wife is already lying flat on a gurney with the nurse by her side. Ash showers down from me as I rush to her. Didn't know you worked cleaning chimneys, the nurse says through a wry smile, and I want to tell her I didn't know we shared such witty intimacy. Instead, I look to my wife, whose eyes are starting to water. I know it's not yet time, she says, but she won't stay inside anymore. She wants out. I take her hand in mine, squeeze it tight, smudging it with runny ash. It's OK, I tell her, then kiss her warm hand, feeling the hardness of the muscles in her arms, We're ready for her. She nods, the first tears escaping her eyes. Staring straight at my face, she says, Your eye, and she can't hold back the surge of more tears. Everything's under control here, the nurse intervenes, Let's deliver this baby. Looking into her phone, she adds that the ambulance is near, Let's get you nice and ready. We all nod and breathe, and when the calm is somewhat restored, I see bits of ash on the gurney and on the floor, Do I have time for a quick shower? While I think I can make out the nurse rolling her eyes, doing her best to look away, my wife says, No, honey, we have to go. Your daughter is on the way. I nod, OK, yes, I say, You're right, just a change of clothes then, and I dash upstairs, where I slide into a fresh T-shirt, wash my ash-smudged face, and pour some water over my hair, which immediately shows oily streaks of black. I lather some soap over my wound, and as I rinse, the wail of the ambulance is loud outside our window. Before my descent, I have a quick look over the mock-up, now complete. The city that will never be.

Downstairs, the nurse counts to three. We lift the gurney and carry my wife through the door to the street. The arborists and the ambulance compete for the top layer of sound. Looking up from the gurney at the falling branches, at the black needles of ash, and at the man slicing through the trees, my wife screams, You idiot, what the fuck are you doing? The man cuts the engine of his chainsaw and looks down, More streetlights, ma'am. My wife's throat muscles clench, and she has to loosen up before speaking, Have you seen the air lately, moron? The man wipes ash from his face, My work, ma'am, gotta eat. The initial stages of another fit begin materializing on her face—a furrowing brow, reddening cheeks, the jerking muscles in her limbs. Get her inside that ambulance, the nurse says, and the paramedics take the gurney from us, sliding her into the back, then signaling for us to get on. With the doors locked and a paramedic at either side of my wife, the ambulance gives a screech, lurches forward, and the siren blares all around us. We sail through the city, through its endless night, parting the traffic, leaving a wake of tire marks and ash behind us. As we soar down Avenida Chapultepec, the paramedics measure my wife's dilation and take her blood pressure. They direct a few stares at my bad eye too, fearsome initially, then drawing the usual morbid smiles. Our nurse is utterly focused, massaging my wife's pineal gland, while I sit back, breathing deeply, shutting my eyes to the white screen behind my lids—a sudden calm in the middle of the storm.

74

The arrival at the hospital delivers a pang fit for the occasion: the urgent beating in my chest renders every object more acutely, even through only one eye. The sacredness of all this dawns on me—it's not just pushing someone out of a body. It's a process, a ritual.

My wife is transferred to a proper hospital gurney, while I fill out some forms with obvious difficulty. Then we are led down a maze of bright corridors all too similar to those when my pterygium was to be removed and I dreamed of clear eyes like my wife dreamed of clear skies—the squeaking wheels of the gurney, the metallic clatter of its structure, a doctor walking beside my wife. Then they vanish behind swinging doors, and I'm allowed no farther while she is prepped.

I'm ordered to stay in the waiting area, where new parents and their relatives anticipate the first look at their newborns, a room where a blue curtain is raised and reveals the insect-like bodies of the infant children: their gray, cloudy eyes, their squirming arms and legs, their lost, confused looks. Ah, the cruelty of it! The healthy newborns safe and sound, while we still have to go through the process. Luckily, not much time passes before two nurses step into the room, one dressed in a white medical gown, the other in violet scrubs. OK, the one wearing white says, louder than needed, though adding the appropriate tinge of urgency, Who's the father? She looks at her notepad and then at everyone in the room. The lack of an immediate response makes her say my name out loud, slowly. I spring from my chair, walk up to them. The nurse in white winces at me, while the other one yanks her head back slightly at the sight of my face, *You're* the father? the nurse in white says, high-pitched, incredulous, and then turning to the other nurse, she adds, Get him his scrubs, then show him to the restroom so he can clean up. I follow her in the direction of the swinging doors, but before we reach them, the nurse in white turns to me, Sir, really scrub yourself with the soap, please. I shrug, Haven't you been outside? The ash is everywhere. She shakes her head, looks briefly to the window, where the moon is a mere suggestion behind the smog and the rushing ash, like my pupil behind the red-speckled, white flesh over my eye. I'm serious, sir. Clean up, and she shows me to the bathroom where, under the white light above the mirror, I notice black streaks of wet soot running from my hairline down my cheeks. Before changing into my scrubs, I wash my face, my wound, anoint myself with sanitizing gel, then make sure my hairnet confines every strand of my hair. My mother was right. I look like a horror movie, but I step out trying to forget my appearance and focus on the task ahead.

When I meet my wife in the delivery room, full of bright lights and cumbia tunes by Celia Cruz, she is already showing the signs of pain: the tight eyes with the skin wrinkling around them, the curled lips, the sibilant fire breaths, the forehead laced with sweat. Her belly seems stouter than usual; she rubs and presses on it as if she could expel our daughter with her own hands. The doctors eye me with caution as I approach the delivery bed, and it takes the nurse's Yes, he is the father, for them to feel at ease. They direct me behind the bed, off my wife's right shoulder. Her skin releases heat like a radiator, her face rosy, fully blushed. The door then swings open, and our pediatrician steps in. He too is covered up in scrubs, his eyes trapped between lines of sky-blue nylon, OK, he says, clutching my wife's toes, Here we go. Are you ready? My wife nods while holding her breath. Looking over to me, the pediatrician stoops back dramatically, Whoa, he says, What happened *to you*? Did not see *that* coming. I try smiling at him but can't. But hey, he says, slipping on transparent latex gloves, Higher stakes here, right? While I nod, he hunkers forward to stare between my wife's open legs, then resurfacing from the sheet covering my wife's lower body, he says, OK, seems like she was up for the late turn. All that bed time paid off. She'll be crowning soon, so we'll try to do this the natural way, OK? And through her pain, my wife can only continue nodding while holding her breath. I'll be performing el tacto now. This'll hurt a little, and he plunges back down like a scuba diver, whistling the tune of "La Vida Es Un Carnaval." I turn to the nurse beside me, who is also mouthing the lyrics to the classic song, Tacto? I ask her. She nods, Exactly what it sounds like, and turning to meet my eyes with what I can tell is nausea, she adds, He, like, pushes his finger inside, and I mean *all the way in,* and touches the baby's head. She touches her own head with her thumb before carrying on, To see how far ahead she is. This also speeds up the contractions, and at that second, my wife screams like I've never heard anyone scream before. It's a guttural screech filling the room, rising well above Celia Cruz's swagger and making my already limited eyesight dim and my legs wobble. Easy now, the nurse says, holding my elbow, leading me to a stool, and handing me a piece of gauze soaked in alcohol to perk me back up. I'm left mostly in a daze nonetheless, staring at the feet shuffling over the white floor of the delivery room. When the pediatrician finishes the tact, my wife seems like she's back to normal, breathing sharply. Come on, man up, the pediatrician tells me, We haven't even started, and all I can do is inhale the scent of the alcohol to, as he put it, man up, and as I do, my senses awaken slightly. Another contraction arrives, and now my wife's breath quickens through her oval-shaped lips. Good, there we go, the pediatrician says, and then turning to me, Feeling better? I nod, gauze still clogging my nostrils. Come over here. Have a look! he says, and I hold on to the bed's railing to lift myself from the stool, moving around my wife with short steps. Go on, the pediatrician points between my wife's legs, and when I crouch to peek in, I see my daughter's head, covered in blood clots and dark hair, like there are no sexual organs there at all. En la madre, I scream out, my pulse slowing, my legs tingling, gooseflesh popping up along every inch of my skin. The pediatrician laughs like a cartoonish villain, What? he says, The head? And I want to say *yes, the head,* but no, it's not the head. It's life inside life, a life I can already feel like my own. It throbs and it breathes, this life. It's coming. Trying to lift my body and reach my wife, thinking of landing a kiss on her forehead and cheering her on through the final stretch, my body goes suddenly cold, and my legs fold under me. Pools of light wobble in front of me before I collapse next to the delivery bed, lights out, a tray with medical tools clattering over me while footsteps rush to my aid. My wife screams *Arthur!* A sound looping through the frayed ends of my mind. The rest happens as if behind the ever-present haze of our sky: *she's crowned. Wait, she's got the umbilical cord wrapped around her neck. Keep an eye on her pressure. OK let's get her out, now, right now.* The words are slightly muffled behind the sound of my thudding heartbeat. Awful thoughts run through my mind as I hear them, thoughts of our daughter's reticence, our daughter who refuses to inhabit this city full of uncertainty and pain, for surely inside the womb, all was good and snug, no fears to face, only the temperate liquid that feeds you, always tucked inside your mother, forever in her contact, and so why would anyone want to come out? Is making a noose from her umbilical cord a final attempt? Like saying *No, not the notion of mortality, not these toxic skies.* Every time I try to stand, a nurse holds me down, and, somehow, amidst this daze, within the beat of Celia Cruz and beeping machines and my wife's moaning, I am aware of my failure to meet what this moment demands of me, which makes me want to cry out, to release every repressed tear, but then there comes a moment—as the CD skips a track, as the machines quiet, as my wife seems to tightly hold her breath—of absolute peace—or is this a hollow, empty quiet? Rolling on to my side, I see the blurry image of the pediatrician holding my daughter's bluish, bloodied, and motionless body, the umbilical cord leading back to my wife. Every second extends. The pulse in my chest is slow, painful. What? my wife screams, What is it? Is she OK? The silence widens, grabs full hold. The image spins, quivers, and ultimately shifts so that all I can see is that ubiquitous, white light.

75

White light all over. I try to lift my body but can't. Celia Cruz's voice returns, jovial and trivial. I rub my eyes with heavy fingers and blink. The blur comes slightly back into shape: I can make out the pediatrician holding my silent daughter, taking her to a table, laying her on her back. I can hear my wife's sobs. I try to meet her eyes but can't. What's happening? I say loudly over the music. Please, in a voice that wavers and implores, that goes into the whitish void—

—Please! my voice and my wife's in unison until, finally, our pleading seems to find a response: from the deep ends of the room comes the disarming shrill of a new voice, shrieks of life and redemption. They're appropriately angry, full of loathing, teeming with hope.

ACKNOWLEDGMENTS

Thank you, Nadine Faraj, Nathlie Provosty, Kara Rooney, and Gryphon Rue, for reading earlier drafts of this novel.

Thank you, Nick Herman, for helping concoct the idea for this novel.

Thank you, Tim MacGabhann, for the many cantina workshops and vegetarian tortas.

Thank you, Maryse Meijer, Christine Stroud, and Autumn House Press.

Thank you, Lu, for the endless support, for your writing on the walls, for running clear, lucid eyes over this text, and for teaching me art through feeling every day.

NEW AND FORTHCOMING RELEASES

Molly by Kevin Honold ♦ Winner of the 2020 Autumn House Fiction Prize, selected by Dan Chaon

The Gardens of Our Childhoods by John Belk ♦ Winner of the 2021 Rising Writer Prize in Poetry, selected by Matthew Dickman

Myth of Pterygium by Diego Gerard Morrison ♦ Winner of the 2021 Rising Writer Prize in Fiction, selected by Maryse Meijer

Out of Order by Alexis Sears ♦ Winner of the 2021 Donald Justice Poetry Prize, selected by Quincy R. Lehr

Queer Nature: A Poetry Anthology, edited by Michael Walsh

Seed Celestial by Sara R. Burnett ♦ Winner of the 2021 Autumn House Poetry Prize, selected by Eileen Myles

Bittering the Wound by Jacqui Germain ♦ Winner of the 2021 CAAPP Book Prize, selected by Douglas Kearney

The Running Body by Emily Pifer ♦ Winner of the 2021 Autumn House Nonfiction Prize, selected by Steve Almond

Entry Level by Wendy Wimmer ♦ Winner of the 2021 Autumn House Fiction Prize, selected by Deesha Philyaw

For our full catalog please visit: http://www.autumnhouse.org